THE GATES OF DISTANCE

THE GATES OF DISTANCE

Sheelagh was very much younger than Luke, though that hadn't stopped her falling in love with him, and in no time the two of them had set off across the world to Luke's romantic island home in the Indian Ocean. The marriage had begun with a terrible misunderstanding – and even after it had been sorted out, could Sheelagh be sure that she was mature enough to cope with all the other difficulties that faced her? With, for instance, the ever-present memory of Luke's dead wife Georgina – and that other menace, the very-much-alive, sophisticated and possessive Viola Whittaker?

The Gates Of Distance

by

Hilary Wilde

Dales Large Print Books
Long Preston, North Yorkshire,
BD23 4ND, England.

British Library Cataloguing in Publication Data.

Wilde, Hilary
    The gates of distance.

    A catalogue record of this book is
    available from the British Library

    ISBN   978-1-84262-689-4 pbk

First published in Great Britain in 1973
by Mills & Boon Limited

Copyright © Hilary Wilde 1973

Cover illustration © Melvyn Warren-Smith by arrangement
with P.W.A. International Ltd.

The moral right of the author has been asserted

Published in Large Print 2009 by arrangement with
The estate of the late Mrs Clare Breton Smith,
care of Juliet Burton Literary Agency

Dales Large Print is an imprint of Library Magna Books Ltd.

Printed and bound in Great Britain by
T.J. (International) Ltd., Cornwall, PL28 8RW

CHAPTER 1

As Sheelagh's father helped her out of the car, lifting her white satin train, keeping the sudden spring wind from blowing her veil about, he smiled at her.

'I'm sure everything will be all right, darling,' he said reassuringly. 'If it isn't, just let me know and I'll see to it.'

Sheelagh Tysack laughed happily. 'I know it'll be all right, Dad,' she told him, looking up at the tall steeple of the centuries-old church and wondering how many brides had been married here.

'You haven't looked too well these last few days,' her father went on. A tall lean man in his mid-sixties, he towered above his daughter. Now as he took her hand, he smiled at her. 'Your mother says all brides get these last-minute blues. Even she did, and she was ten years older than you are when we got married.'

Poor Dad, Sheelagh was thinking, he was trying hard to be cheerful, for they had always been so close, playing golf together, gardening, discussing politics, so he was going to miss her. Never had he approved of any of her boy-friends, and although at one time it had worried her because he didn't seem to like Luke, she had soon realised that no matter whom she married, her father wouldn't think him good enough!

They joined the bridesmaids, Jess and Pauline, her two old school friends, who smiled at her. Tom, an usher, was also in the chancel.

'You look smashing,' Jess, her red hair for once disciplined under the big floppy pale green hat, said.

'On time, too,' Pauline teased, her short brown curls escaping from under her green hat. 'Your dress is lovely, Sheelagh.'

The usher, Tom Jackson, was asking Sheelagh's father a question and suddenly a short plump woman in a very elegant-looking deep blue silk suit came to Sheelagh's side.

'Excuse me,' she said, and began to straighten the train of the white silk bridal gown, then looked at Sheelagh, whose large dark eyes were puzzled. 'I must just put the veil straight,' the short plump woman, who seemed about to burst out of the seams of her suit, murmured, pushing past the bridesmaids and moving in close to Sheelagh.

A little puzzled, then deciding it must be someone sent from the dressmaker who had made the gown, Sheelagh stood still. The woman's mouth was very near Sheelagh's ear and suddenly the woman said softly:

'Luke's taste has improved. You're much prettier than his first wife.'

She spoke so softly that Sheelagh was certain that no one, not even her father by her side who was still talking to Tom, could have heard, and then the unknown woman seemed to slide away quietly, vanishing back in the church.

Sheelagh had a strange feeling – not exactly as if she was going to faint, but she turned quickly to her father, sliding her hand through his arm, grateful for the warmth of his hand as it closed over hers and he turned to her.

'Sheelagh,' he said, sounding shocked. 'What's wrong, darling? You look terrible.'

Somehow, she never knew how, Sheelagh managed a smile.

'Just wedding-day blues, Dad,' she told him.

Tom was looking inside the church; he turned and nodded his head and they could hear the rolling rhythm of the organ.

11

'You're sure you'll be all right?' her father asked anxiously.

'Quite sure,' she promised, and then the long, slow, seemingly endless walk down the aisle began.

Everyone was standing, singing the hymn she had chosen, many looking round expectantly as the twenty-year-old bride walked down the aisle, holding on to her father's arm tightly.

It was like a nightmare dream to Sheelagh. Her limbs moved automatically, but she wasn't even aware of what she was doing, for her thoughts were milling round her head unhappily.

It couldn't be true, for Luke had never told her. Why hadn't he told her? Luke was thirty-five, so it wouldn't be surprising if he had been married before. But what hurt her was the thought that he hadn't told her. Surely when you love someone you have no secrets? And then her fingers clutched her father's even tighter, but she didn't see his anxious face as he turned to look at her, for her thoughts had gone far away, remembering how about three days earlier, the phone bell had rung and she had answered it. A strange voice, slightly lilting, rather Welsh in tone, asked:

'Is Luke there?'

'I'm afraid he isn't, but he'll be down here tomorrow,' Sheelagh had said. 'Can I give him a message for you?'

'Don't bother. My name's Viola Whittaker. I've known Luke for years. I thought he knew my address, but I've had no invitation to the wedding. Will it be all right if I come?'

'Of course,' Sheelagh had said quickly, delighted that a friend of Luke's was coming, for her mother had remarked several times that it was strange that Luke had so few friends to invite. Luke had said that to him marriage was a private affair, so you only asked your *real* friends, not just acquaintances. 'I'm sure he'll be pleased,' Sheelagh had added.

'Where is the wedding and the reception?' the lilting voice asked, and Sheelagh told her.

The next day when Luke had arrived and taken her in his arms, she had forgotten everything but her love for him and it was several hours later that she had remembered.

'Luke, I forgot, but an old friend of yours phoned to ask if she could come to the wedding,' she had said.

Luke had looked up. He was slowly filling his pipe. Now he frowned. 'A friend of mine?'

13

'Yes, I think ... I think her name was Viola... Viola...'

And Luke had jumped up. 'Oh hell! Not Viola Whittaker?'

'That's right, Luke. I said I was sure you'd be delighted and I told her where it ... was...' Sheelagh's voice had slowly dwindled away as she stared at him. Never, never in the months she had known him had she seen him so angry. His hands were clenched, his face a dull red as he stared at her.

'You had no right...' he began.

'I'm sorry, Luke. She said you were an old friend and...' Sheelagh had been startled and even a little frightened at the way he was fighting to control his anger.

Then he smiled. 'Don't worry. It's not your fault. It's just that woman'

'Darling!' Sheelagh's father was now saying urgently. 'We're nearly there.'

Sheelagh, looking round her, saw a mass of faces, staring at her curiously. She forced herself to smile at her father, but she could not forget Luke's unexpected anger, for it had made her realise how little she really knew him. But what was worrying her now was the fact that the lilting voice on the phone had been the voice of the woman who had spoken to her in the chancel.

14

'Luke's taste has improved. You're much prettier than his first wife.'

The words stung in her ears – and then suddenly she saw Luke.

He was standing by Cary, the best man, and now Luke, tall, well-built with broad shoulders, a sun-tanned skin and short blond hair, slowly turned his head and smiled at her.

It was as if she had let a cloak, that had been heavy on her shoulders, fall to the ground as her body and limbs came to life and her smile was natural.

Luke darling, she thought, I love you so much, so very much.

From that moment everything was different. She could look around her, admiring the beautiful flowers on the altar, the friendly smile of the clergyman. Glancing sideways at her father, she saw that he had noticed the change in her too, because he smiled back happily.

She suddenly understood everything. This Viola woman was not a friend of Luke's. Quite the opposite, in fact. She hated him and what she had said had been a malicious lie. It had been stupid even for one moment to believe what such a woman had said.

The wonder of the moment seemed to

envelop her – the beauty of the church, the sincerity in the clergyman's voice as he spoke of love and hope and trusting one another. She felt ashamed, then, and wished she could turn and throw her arms round Luke's neck and apologise for having believed that dreadful woman, even for a moment.

The words went round and round in her head again, but this time they were different words. 'Dearly beloved...' 'In sickness and in health,' beautiful words that meant so much more than they sounded. She didn't even have a moment of nervousness when it was her turn to speak. Her voice came clear and certain as she said what she should. She glanced up at the man by her side and saw the love in Luke's eyes and knew that she had been stupid to feel upset and that everything was going to be all right.

When the final words were said and they stood there, man and wife, she turned impulsively to Luke. She saw in his eyes the passion she felt, the longing to be held so tightly she could hardly breathe, to feel his strong hands stroke her hair, trace the bones in her face gently and then the feeling of his mouth hard against hers. It was as if Luke read her thoughts, for as he stooped to kiss her lightly, he whispered: 'Later, my love.

Later...' and she smiled at him, loving him with all her heart.

Just the feel of his warm hand on her arm as they went to the vestry to sign the register made her so happy she wanted to sing. She was Luke's wife. Luke was her husband. Now they could be together, all day and all night; now they could make their home, spend the rest of their lives together.

She bent down and signed her name.

Then there were kisses all round and the organ began to play the joyous, almost triumphant sound of the Wedding March.

Her arm through Luke's, his hand tightly round hers, Sheelagh walked down the aisle. Smiling at her mother, who was dabbing her eyes with her hankie, smiling at her father whose smile was obviously fixed, wishing Luke's parents could have been there.

Suddenly she realised that she didn't know where his family lived, if indeed they were still alive. All she knew was that his father, an Australian, had married a South African woman and that was how it was Luke had spent most of his youth in Swaziland. Luke never wanted to discuss what he called the Forgotten Past. He seemed even to hate it.

Smiling, Sheelagh suddenly saw the woman she hated so much, the malicious liar. She was standing at the end of the pew, smiling, a sceptical, cynical smile. She nodded her head as she caught Sheelagh's eyes.

It was as if a cold piece of ice had gone sliding down Sheelagh's spine, for there was something frightening about the woman, something evil. And then they were outside the church, posing as the cameras clicked and the professional photographer made them stand in different positions for their photos to be taken, then her parents had to come and stand with them.

The confetti fluttered, half blinding her, as she and Luke fought their way through the crowd of guests to the waiting car with its white ribbon telling the world that this was a newly married couple.

As the car drew away from the kerb, covered with confetti, Luke turned to her and took her in his arms.

'At last,' he said. 'I wondered just how long I could wait.'

His kiss seemed to go on for ever and she forgot the horrible woman who had lied to her. She forgot everything but that she loved Luke and was his wife.

Sheelagh's home, built high on the Downs above Eastbourne with a superb view of the

English Channel, was large, but even so, with all the guests to the reception, it seemed crowded. Luke and Sheelagh took their places at the head table, while her father sat next to her and her mother sat on the other side of Luke.

It was funny, Sheelagh was thinking, that while her father disapproved of her boy-friends, her mother had always encouraged them. She had even liked Tony Rogers, though that affair had not lasted for long. Now she was chatting away happily to Luke, leaving Sheelagh to talk to her father.

'What was wrong with you, darling, at the church?' he asked anxiously.

Sheelagh hesitated. She was tempted to tell him about the unpleasant woman, but then she decided not to. Her father didn't approve of Luke and this might only make things worse, especially if it happened to be true.

Glancing quickly at Luke with his good-humoured expression, his sudden infectious laugh, his perfect manners, Sheelagh knew that if Luke had been married before and had deliberately not told her, there must be a good reason for it. She loved him so she must trust him. Not that she minded if he was married before, but it hurt her to think he hadn't told her. When you love there should be no secrets.

'Sheelagh,' her father said quietly, 'aren't you listening to me? I asked you what went wrong in church?'

With a jerk, Sheelagh returned to the reception, glancing round her at the huge white vases of lilies and bright red flowers.

They were all in the lofty hall with the graceful curved staircase leading to the bedrooms. Everywhere there were small tables with the guests sitting down and being served a light lunch. Champagne was being poured into glasses, everyone was laughing and talking, occasionally glancing at the head table as if expecting the speeches to begin. At least there was no sign of that horrible woman, Sheelagh thought, wondering if she ought to tell Luke now and then deciding not to until they had left her parents and gone to start their life together.

'Sheelagh!' There was an anxious note in her father's voice and she turned at once.

'I'm sorry, Dad, I was miles away.' She smiled at him and he thought he had never seen his daughter look so beautiful, so lovely that it was like a knife cutting out his heart, for he wanted her to be happy. She was far too good for this brash giant who towered above her, for little Sheelagh was only five feet and one inch high! Was Luke Jessop going to be a good husband? John Tysack was thinking worriedly. He had better be! John Tysack felt the anger growing inside him and knew he must control it. If Sheelagh loved the man...

'You looked quite ill, Sheelagh. I thought you were going to faint,' John Tysack said.

She smiled. 'I thought I was, too. Just nerves, Dad – as Mum said. It all seems rather overpowering, a church filled with people looking at you, that endless walk down the aisle. I had no idea it was so long. I began to think we'd never get there!'

John Tysack smiled, suddenly happy, for this was his real Sheelagh, chatting like a child, with that happy laugh. Indeed he had found the walk down the aisle all too short, for at the other end of the walk, he had to hand her over to another man, a man about whom they knew very little, a man much too old for Sheelagh.

'Dad, please!' Sheelagh's hand was on his. 'Don't look as if the end of the world has come. I'll be visiting you. We'll play golf ... you can come and advise me about my garden.'

'Luke has bought a house?' John Tysack

asked quickly. That had been another of his problems. Where, just where were they going to live? Would it be far away or conveniently near?

Sheelagh shrugged. 'I honestly don't know, Dad. Luke always says that we'll worry about that when we come back. Just think, Dad, we're going to Italy, the Greek Islands, Spain and perhaps Austria. Luke says we'll stay as long as we like anywhere. No rushing. We'll have a car, and he's used to driving on the Continent...'

Cary, the best man, glanced down the table. It was time for the speeches, which he introduced. They were soon over. Sheelagh's eyes were stinging with tears as she heard her father's usually firm voice waver a little as he talked of the sacrifice he was making, allowing his only child to marry. There was laughter, because he smiled, but Sheelagh knew he meant it. Luke's speech was short but confident as he thanked everyone and said how happy he was.

He was happy, Sheelagh thought, then what about her? Never in her life had she been so happy. Now he turned to her and took her hand and it was as if they were quite alone and the huge crowded hall empty.

Then came the cutting of the cake with

much laughter, for little five-foot Sheelagh looked almost like a pygmy standing by the giant who was her husband. Sheelagh battled with the knife in vain and then Luke's strong hand closed over hers and the cake was cut effortlessly.

Afterwards they had to circulate. There were very few friends of Luke's, but he introduced her to them and there was laughter and chatter. The noise seemed terrible to Sheelagh and she longed for it to be over and she and Luke speeding away. She saw Luke glancing at his wrist watch, so she knew he felt the same. Finally when it was felt the bride and groom had done their duty, Jess and Pauline came to her to say it was time she changed. They went with her up the curved staircase, along the corridor to her bedroom. It had been her bedroom since she was a baby, since she had never lived anywhere except in this big dignified and gracious house.

'I'll manage,' Sheelagh said, knowing the two girls had boy-friends waiting for them downstairs. 'I'll be okay.'

Her trousseau was packed and waiting in the car. Her going-away dress was hanging from the top of her wardrobe. It was a pale yellow crimplene dress, not too thin, for though it was late spring, the days could be chilly, and she had a matching linen coat. She looked in the mirror at her long black hair, elaborately twisted round her head, and frowned. Luke liked her hair to hang down her back so that he could twist it round his hands and gently pull it, laughing when she pretended it hurt as they played the caveman game. Now she brushed it out, tying it back with a small piece of gold ribbon. She changed her shoes to more comfortable ones, then took a last look at herself.

'Mrs Luke Jessop...' she told herself. 'Sheelagh Jessop. Sounds good!'

She laughed happily, leaving her wedding dress and veil to be put away by her old nanny, who now acted as their domestic help.

Outside in the corridor, Sheelagh stopped dead, as if by some heavy obstacle. Indeed that was how it felt, because that awful woman, Viola something-or-other, was waiting for her, standing in the way, her face flushed, her eyes narrow.

'You don't believe me, do you?' she demanded, glaring at Sheelagh. 'You think I'm a liar. Well, I'm not. Georgina was my best friend. I loved her. She wasn't beautiful, she had a big nose, but she was happy, always laughing. Until she married Luke.

He took her to the loneliest spot in the world and used to leave her there alone She was terrified. You're a fool to have married him. He's the most selfish egoist I've ever met. He'll kill you as he killed Georgina.'

Sheelagh found her voice. 'I don't believe it! Luke's not like that.'

The woman laughed, an ugly sound. 'That's what you think! You don't know the real Luke. What sort of man can he be when he's never even seen his own child?'

'His child?' This time Sheelagh's voice was shocked.

'Yes, his child. What sort of man can he be?'

'I ... I...' Sheelagh began, and then she saw her father's tall, lean body coming down the corridor. 'All right, Dad,' she called. 'I'm coming!'

She pushed her way past the woman, feeling sick with dismay, running down the corridor, feeling tempted to throw herself into her father's arms and telling him everything. Could it be true? Could Luke be like that? Could he be so totally indifferent to his own child? A child who needed a father?

'No hurry, but Luke's getting impatient,' her father said cheerfully. 'You look very nice, darling.'

'So do you.' Sheelagh hugged him hard. 'I'm going to miss you, Dad.'

He stifled a sigh. 'We'll miss you, too, my dear, but there it is. You had to grow up one day. I just hope you're happy.'

'Why don't you like Luke, Dad?' Sheelagh asked. As they reached the staircase and stared down at the groups of guests waiting expectantly for the bride to toss her bouquet, she remembered.

'My bouquet, Dad. I've forgotten it!'

'I'll get it,' he said quickly, and then she thought of that awful woman, still in the corridor, quite capable of stopping her father and telling him everything. Even if it was a lie, and it must be a lie, she thought, it could only upset her father, especially at a time like this.

'I will, Dad.' Sheelagh let go of him and ran down the corridor. Thankfully she saw it was empty. That horrible woman had vanished somewhere. If only she had never come! If only ... if only, Sheelagh thought. Why should that woman make up so many lies, if they were lies? Yet they must be. They simply must be, she thought, as she almost tripped over her shoes in her bedroom and grabbed the bouquet of yellow roses.

It couldn't be true. It mustn't be, she was

thinking as she ran back down the corridor to join her father. She loved Luke too much...

As she walked down the stairs, her father holding her hand, the guests clapped excitedly. Halfway down, Sheelagh tossed the bouquet. She heard Pauline's cry of triumph as she caught it, but after that she forgot everything else but the look on the face of the man who was waiting for her. Luke, whom she loved so much. That woman must have been lying, must have been.

Impulsively, Sheelagh turned to her father. 'Bless you, Dad,' she said, her voice uneven. 'I'd like us to get away quickly. I'll write.'

'I know you will. Come on!' He took her arm and they hurried down the stairs to where Luke waited.

CHAPTER 2

The journey to London in the large white Mercedes took a surprisingly short time, for Luke knew the countryside well and drove Sheelagh down the lanes rather than along the crowded highways. They hardly spoke.

Sheelagh, with her shoes kicked off and her feet tucked under her, rested against Luke's arm as he drove. The sun was still shining and the country beautiful with its flower-covered fruit trees and gardens bright with spring colour.

Luke had to wake her when they reached their hotel, which was just outside London and where they planned to spend the night and fly off on their honeymoon next day.

'Are you tired?' he asked, his voice gentle.

She smiled sleepily. 'I am a bit.'

'I've some phoning to do. Why not shower and have a sleep? I'll be back in an hour,' Luke suggested.

Stifling a yawn, Sheelagh smiled. 'Sounds a good idea.'

It was a pleasant hotel; luxurious without being oppressive. Their suite – for Luke had booked one, saying they would dine alone and avoid the outside world – was delightful; the lounge had a wide couch, deep comfortable armchairs, thin see-through gold curtains so that you could look at the great open park below them.

The *good idea* failed to work, Sheelagh realised later. She had showered, lain on the huge double bed, and closed her eyes. But sleep had not come. Instead she found her-

28

self hearing that smug cruel voice saying: 'He'll kill you as he killed Georgina.'

Why had that woman lied like that? What was the point? Did she hate Luke and was she trying to wreck his marriage? Yet she must have known that such lies could be proved to be lies, so what real harm could she do?

But were they lies? Sheelagh wondered, as she tossed and turned on the bed. And if they were, *why* had he lied to her?

If he loved her, surely his past life could be shared with her? And if it was true he had a child ... that was another thing that made her doubt, Sheelagh thought unhappily, for Luke wasn't that kind of man. He liked children, he got on well with them. That had been proved when her cousin Netta, married and with four children all under seven years of age, had come to visit them and Luke had played with them for hours, obviously quite happy. A man who loved children would never ignore his own child. That must be a lie, too. In fact, it was all a pack of lies, she thought, as she jumped up, quickly dressed, carefully brushed out her long dark hair so that it hung like a cloud round her face. She loved Luke and that was all that mattered.

She was in the sitting-room, watching all the lights of the nearby town sparkling, when Luke came back. He looked tired, but he bent over her as she lay curled up on the couch, and kissed her.

'I feel a mess,' he confessed. 'I'll have a quick shower. I've ordered dinner and drinks. See you in a moment,' he finished, and vanished into the bedroom.

A tiny shiver went through her. Those words were so typical of Luke, yet somehow she had never noticed until that day that he never asked her what she *wanted* to eat, he always ordered what he thought she would like.

He was so sure of himself, so certain that he knew what was right for her, but was he always right? And would he be always right? She had never realised this before. Now it made her see just how little she knew of him.

Not that it had been a rush engagement. They had met at her uncle's diamond wedding party in Hampstead. She had been rather bored, as most of the guests were in her parents' age group, and then suddenly this huge giant of a man had strode across the crowded room and asked her if she would like to dance as the younger generation, few though they were, were organising it in another room. Later she had laughed when he joked about their difference in size, but she had liked him from that first moment. Perhaps, even, loved?

She hadn't seen him after that for two months and then one day he turned up at their house, reminded her of how they had met, and asked her out to dinner. She had gone, although conscious of her father's anxious frown and feeling a little amused, for after all, she *was* nineteen and no helpless child, aware also of her mother's approval.

It had been at dinner that Luke had told her frankly that he had tried to forget her. He had rested his square chin on his hands and looked at her thoughtfully.

'You see, I don't want to fall in love with you. A, you're much too young and I'm much too much older than you. B, I'm not very keen to get married. So I tried to forget you. But I can't. So I thought I'd better see you and maybe I'd...'

'Be disillusioned?' she had suggested with a pseudo-meekness.

He had looked grave. 'Exactly. Unfortunately I'm not.' And suddenly his hand, so much bigger than hers, had closed over her fingers. 'I'm afraid I do love you after all,' he had said slowly.

'I'm sorry.' She had tried to joke, but he refused to let her.

'It's not your fault, Sheelagh. Nor is it mine. It's just one of those things. But I'm not sure I'll make a good husband.'

Now, as she listened to the running water in the bathroom, she remembered those words which, at the time, she had hardly noticed.

'I'm not sure I'll make a good husband,' he had said.

Then was that horrible woman right? Had he already been a bad husband?

At that moment the bathroom door opened and Luke came in, looking even taller than usual in his long grey trousers and dark red velvet jacket, his hair still wet from the shower.

Without realising what she was going to say, Sheelagh turned her head.

'Why didn't you tell me you'd been married before?' she asked.

Luke stood still, frowning. 'I thought everyone knew.'

'I didn't. Luke, I can't understand why you didn't tell me.'

He came to stand by her side, towering above her.

'Because it was of no importance. It's in

the past and better forgotten.'

She sat up, clasping her knees, her eyes puzzled.

'But, Luke darling...'

He jerked the chair from in front of the writing desk and straddled it. 'You didn't tell me you were engaged to Tony Rogers once.'

She felt her cheeks go hot. 'It was only for two months, and then I knew...'

'My marriage lasted six months, but I knew on the second day why she had married me, and that was the end. She believed I was wealthy, the heir of a millionaire who was merely being kind and helpful to me.' He smiled – a strange smile, one she had never seen before. 'Do you want a dossier of my life?'

Sheelagh shivered. 'Not really, but ... but Luke, I know so little about you.'

'All right,' he said, standing up, kicking the chair out of the way and coming to pick her up in his arms. 'But first I'm going to kiss you.'

As his mouth came down on hers, she struggled, turning her head away, stiffening her body even though she longed to hold him close, to say that they would forget it and even if he had murdered his wife, it didn't matter. Nothing mattered but that she loved him.

She was startled when he dropped her on the couch. She lay, spread-eagled, staring up at the stranger who was leaning over her, his eyes bright with fury, his face red.

'I suppose Viola has been talking,' he said. 'And you believed her.'

He strode towards the window and she wished he would come back. She sat up, trembling. 'I'm sorry, Luke darling. It doesn't matter ... nothing matters but that I love you.'

He swung round, his whole body trembling with the desire for the violence he was controlling. 'That's a lie. If you loved me, you wouldn't have listened to her. And if you had to, then you wouldn't have believed it. I suppose she told you I killed my wife?'

There was a gentle knock on the door and in came the waiter, carrying a tray with drinks on it. When he had gone, there was an awkward silence. Luke poured out the drinks, took hers to Sheelagh, and then went and sat down, folding his arms, his face grave as he looked at her. She gazed back, her hand unsteady as she sipped the liquid. If only she had never said that ... if only...

'You're right,' Luke began. 'We know far too little about one another, although we've been engaged for a whole year.'

'You know all about me,' Sheelagh told him.

'On the contrary, I know very little about you. Few girls today of twenty are content to live at home with their parents, having no career, showing no desire to *live*. How come you were like this?'

'I never thought about it.' Sheelagh looked puzzled. 'Somehow it just happened.'

'A real daddy's pet!' Luke sneered.

Sheelagh's cheeks were hot. 'I'm not!'

'Oh yes, you are – precocious and spoilt. You've no idea what life in the outer world is like. That's why I fought loving you. I couldn't see how we could complement one another. You need protection, security. I hate the words. I love danger.' He laughed – a strange laugh. 'You should never have married me.'

'Why tell me that now? If you knew it why did you marry me?' Sheelagh asked.

She was unprepared for his quick movements, but the next second he was kneeling by her side, his arms like bands of steel round her, his mouth hard on her mouth. Then just as suddenly he let her go and she lay back, breathless, while he strode round the room.

'That's why I married you. Because I love

you. Because I can't get you out of my ... oh, hell!' He sat down abruptly. 'Where were we? Oh, yes, you were going to tell me why you stayed at home and didn't get a job.'

'Well ... well...' Sheelagh twisted her fingers together, hanging her head so that her hair swung forward, hiding her face from him. 'I wasn't very bright at school except where languages were concerned and I find them as easy as anything. Then the year I left, Mum was taken ill – arthritis or something. Anyhow, I looked after her and then ... well, somehow when she got better, I just stayed at home. Mum and Dad were quite old when they had me, Mum was thirty-eight and Dad forty-seven, so by the time I was nineteen he was retired and pretty miserable. That's how it came about that he taught me golf and bridge and I helped him in the garden. He'd always been used to people around him and he hated being on his own.'

'He had your mother.'

'Mum?' Sheelagh found she could laugh, could even toss back her hair and look at him. 'Mum sits on every committee there is in the district. She travels around, giving talks, and loves it. Just because Dad's retired she doesn't want to give up her full life. In any case, she loathes golf, bridge and gardening.'

'I see.' Luke sounded thoughtful and Sheelagh wondered why. 'And this Tony Rogers? You didn't tell me about him.'

Her cheeks burned. 'That was a stupid mistake on my part and I'd rather...'

'I'd rather hear about it,' Luke snapped, rising to refill her glass and his. 'I don't think I've met him.'

'No. He's in America at the moment.'

'What happened?' Luke gave her the glass and went and sat down.

'It was nothing really. Tony had lived in the next house to ours for ever. I mean, he lived there before I was born – he's six years older than me, and we sort of grew up together. I always felt ... well, is relaxed the word? with him. Then Mum began to talk about my settling down, marrying and giving them some grandchildren while they were young enough to enjoy them, and ... I thought of marriage and...'

'You didn't like the idea,' Luke finished for her.

Startled, Sheelagh stared at him. 'How did you know?'

'It's obvious. Anything that removes you from the protective arms of your father frightens you.'

Her cheeks were red. 'That's not true!'

'Yes, it is. So long as your father is near, you feel safe. So long as you're near him, you'll never be you. You're your father's shadow, baby,' Luke said scornfully. 'It's time you grew up and threw away your nappy.'

Sheelagh sat up angrily. 'That's absolute tripe! I love Dad, but I'm not dependent on him at all.'

'Is that so?' he sneered, his eyes cold. It was as if his eyes had withdrawn, were looking at something else. 'So you got engaged to the boy next door, feeling safe with him.'

'Well, at least I *knew* him. I was used to his moods and ... and ... well, I knew him. And then ... well, I don't know quite why, but I suddenly knew I didn't love him and that marriage without love could be...'

'Hell,' again Luke provided the word.

A gentle tap on the door and dinner arrived. A delicious meal, Sheelagh thought, for if she had ordered it herself, it couldn't have been more to her taste. What a memory Luke must have to know all her favourite dishes! Prawn cocktail, grilled sole, chocolate sauce on ice cream and champagne to drink to each other.

They laughed and chatted, but behind it all

was a stiffness that Sheelagh feared, a stiffness that could come between them. Luke still had not told her *anything.* But was it so important? If only she had kept her mouth shut!

After dinner, she sat on the couch, drinking her coffee, Luke opposite her, his voice cold again.

'So you came to your senses and dumped Tony Rogers.'

'Yes. It was ... it was horrible.' She shivered, remembering Tony's face, his dismay, then his anger. The way her father had been disappointed for, as he said, it was going to be so nice to have his married daughter as a neighbour. Only her mother had been on her side. 'Tony,' she had said, 'was not for you. You need someone strong, someone on whom you can lean.'

'So...' Luke said thoughtfully, 'that was over. Then we met.' He smiled. 'Did you love me at sight?'

Sheelagh stared at him. 'I'm ... I'm not sure. I did like you. You were a good dancer and...'

'But if I had never turned up at your house, you would have forgotten me?' Luke's words were as hard as his voice. He waited for her answer.

She shook her head slowly, her long black hair swinging. 'I would never have forgotten you, but...' The rest of her words were smothered as he moved swiftly, kneeling by her, gathering her in his arms, his lips kissing her eyes, her mouth, her neck. Then, as before, he suddenly let go of her so that she fell back on the cushions and he was walking about the room, his hands clutched behind his back, his head thrust forward, his voice hoarse.

'Now it's my turn to dig out the skeletons from the family wardrobe. My father was an Australian. He met my mother when she was visiting a relation in Perth. They married, and when I was four years old, we all went to Swaziland where my mother had been born. Her parents had a big citrus orchard there. Of course I can't remember much, but they were both killed in a train smash. Then I was tossed from aunt to aunt, feeling and being allowed to know that I was a nuisance. I was seventeen when I got fed up with the situation and got myself a job. I went from job to job, learning a little here, a little there. It was pretty grim, but infinitely better than to live where I wasn't wanted. Then I met a fellow – a weird sort of bloke, bald as could be, deep-set eyes, one of them glass. Made you think he was squinting. Ach, man, but he had brains. I worked for him. I learned that he was all but a millionaire. He had a filthy temper, but that didn't worry me. We got on. Quite a few exciting things were happening about that time, the finding of minerals which promised a good future, the future too of the tourist market. We moved to Madagascar. Then I met Georgina.'

He paused, going to stand by the window, talking over his shoulder, his voice curt as if what he was doing was disagreeable.

'I was pretty lonely. Georgina had no brains and no beauty, but she was always laughing. She never read anything or listened to the radio or took an interest in my work. All she wanted was money. It was the day after we were married that I learned the truth. She had believed I was old Mercury's heir. When I said he was just a pal and we were always having fights, I thought she'd black out. She accused me of deceiving her, of lying. I hadn't. I knew that one day I'd be as rich as old Mercury.'

He paused, went to pour himself a drink and then swung round.

'I am nearly, now. However, Mercury had given me a good job on an island in the Comoro Archipelago. They're beautiful, fascinating, and with a terrific future. He'd found a small one of little apparent use, and offered me a share in it. I had a little money saved, so I went in. I knew – and it's since been proved – that he was right.'

'Comoro Archipelago? Where on earth is it?'

'Between Northern Mozambique and Madagascar. In the Indian Ocean, there's a deep sea trench and from here these strange mysterious islands rise as peaks of a mountain range. It's beautiful, fascinating and primitive. Georgina hated it, but it was my job. In six months she left me. She refused to come back.'

'But why?'

'I never knew. She called it a jungle. I think she expected a white marble palace – I don't know.' He walked to look out of the window again. 'I just don't know. I had to stay on the island, it was part of our contract. I hadn't much money either as I was investing it as I earned it. Anyhow, she went.'

'And had your child?'

He swung round. 'Yes, my child. Viola told you everything? I can imagine! That I killed my wife and neglected my child. Right?'

Sheelagh moved uneasily as he looked at her, his eyes furious.

'She ... she said you'd never seen your child.'

'It shows how little that old cow knows. The truth is I've seen her quite often, but she hasn't seen me.'

'But why? Your own child?'

'Yes, my own child.' He turned to the window again. 'Zoe – that's her name – was eighteen months old when Georgina died. I didn't even know she was ill. It was very sudden. Then her mother wrote to me, telling me, because of course I'd been sending Georgina money.' He swung round again. 'Oh, yes, I kept my wife. I don't suppose Viola told you that! It meant I had practically nothing left, but I managed. Anyhow, my mother-in-law wrote to tell me. She asked me to leave the child with them. She begged me not to take the child away. It was bad enough, she said, that Zoe's mother had died. It was unfair to the child, this constant movement.'

He sighed and came to straddle the chair near Sheelagh.

'I knew all about that – the misery of having no home, no security. I wondered how I would cope with an eighteen-month-old child, living as I did, never sure from one day to the next where Mercury was sending me. So I agreed. Mrs Hamilton, Georgina's mother, was grateful. It was she who suggested that I could see Zoe but asked me not to let the child see me. I agreed. I've paid for her schooling and everything, naturally. She loves her grandparents. When it was suggested she should go to boarding school she was quite hysterical. She's happier with them than she would ever be with me.'

'I think you were right,' Sheelagh said slowly, trying to ignore the truth she had faced: that Luke *had* loved Georgina, despite what he had said, for his voice had changed completely when he said: '....when Georgina died.' He still loved her, he had not forgotten her. 'But it's different now,' Sheelagh went on slowly. 'You have me.'

'Have I?' Luke asked.

'Of course you have. We could make a home for Zoe. I think she should have her father.'

'Just because you love your father? All girls don't feel the same.'

'I think they do.'

'You think!' he said scornfully. 'What do you know of the world? – pampered, protected by your father.'

She realised suddenly that they were very near a quarrel. On their wedding night, too.

'I could be wrong,' she began.

Luke looked at her. 'So could I, I suppose.' He stood up. 'Well? Are you satisfied? Or do you still believe I killed my wife and deserted my child?'

'I didn't believe it.'

'Didn't you? Then why did you ask all those questions?'

'Because ... because...' She sat up, her long dark hair swinging, her eyes anxious.

'Exactly. Because,' he said sarcastically. 'A fine way to start a marriage. Bride suspects groom of murder and child desertion.'

'I didn't suspect you!'

'Then why, as I said before, did you ask all those questions?'

'Because...'

'Look,' he said angrily. 'Cut out the becauses. I'm fed up to the teeth with them. You didn't trust me – let's face the truth. You preferred to believe what that...' He stood up and turned away. 'Well, that's over, anyhow, or so I presume. Or would you like further details?'

Sheelagh stood up. 'Luke, please ... please! It was just that I realised how little I knew about you, and wanted to know more.'

'Well, you know now. I was a fool eleven years ago and married the wrong person. I have a daughter who is happier with her grandparents than she would be with me. So I'm blamed for both things. Okay, if that's how you feel about it.' He looked at his watch. 'Hell, look at the time! We'd better go to bed. I've got some phone calls to make, so the bathroom's yours. I won't be long.'

He walked across the room and out of the door, closing it with a small but sufficiently angry bang. Sheelagh stood very still. How different everything was proving from what she had expected! Quarrelling, his angry sarcastic voice, his cold, hard eyes. Surely he could understand? She loved him, so she had wanted to know all about his life.

She bathed and put on her specially bought pale pink shortie nightie and jacket. She sat on the edge of the bed and waited, her eyes on the clock. It was nearly midnight. Who could Luke be phoning at this hour of the night?

It seemed hours that she sat there, waiting for Luke. She wondered if she should get into bed, but she was so tired she knew she would fall asleep, and this might anger him still more.

Nearly two hours later, he came in, his face flushed, his eyes narrowed. 'Sorry I was so long. You shouldn't have waited up for me,' he said curtly.

'Luke, I want to tell you something,' she said, standing up, realising how important this was.

'You do? Why waste words? Actions are far better,' he said, and before she knew what was happening she was in his arms, sprawled across the bed, his mouth kissing her neck, her arms, his hands running over her hair. 'Let's forget the past,' he muttered, leaning over her. 'It's done for. Only the present counts.'

'But Zoe...' Sheelagh gasped, hardly able to breathe. 'We can't forget your child.'

'We'll have children of our own,' he said, and roughly pushed back her head so that he could kiss the nape of her neck. 'This is our life, Sheelagh.'

She felt herself stiffen. What sort of man was he who could toss aside his own child, the child who had no mother and who needed a father?

Luke must also have felt her stiffen, for he let go of her, and stood up, scowling down.

'Go to bed, Sheelagh,' he said as if speaking to a child. He picked up his pyjamas and dressing-gown, both laid out on the side of the bed, and a pillow. 'I'll have a quick shower and sleep in the sitting-room.'

'But ... but...' Her eyes wide with shock,

47

Sheelagh stared at him.

'But me no buts, child,' he said scornfully. 'I refuse to make love to a lump of ice. Goodnight.'

He strode to the bathroom and closed the door. Sheelagh crawled into bed, put out the light and closed her eyes tightly and listened to the running of the water in the bathroom. When he came out, she thought, she would run into his arms, cry and tell him how sorry she was. Whatever happened, she must save their marriage. How could she have been so stupid? Sudden great sobs were racking her body while the tears chased down her cheeks.

When next she opened her eyes, she was not alone in bed. Luke lay by her side, propped up by pillows, reading a newspaper and drinking coffee.

'Good morning,' he said casually. 'Your coffee must be getting cold. I tried to wake you, but you were sound asleep.'

She looked at him, puzzled. How long had he lain by her side? How could she have gone to sleep? The last she could remember was listening to the water in the bathroom and fighting the tears that had run down her cheeks.

'Like part of the paper?' he asked, taking out a couple of pages and passing them to her. 'Mustn't be too long, because we've got to get to the airport earlier than I thought.'

'Thank ... thank you,' Sheelagh said, sitting up, plumping her pillows, holding the paper in one hand as she lifted the coffee cup with the other. There was silence as he read the paper. Sheelagh didn't know what to do. It was just as if they had been married for fifty years and had lost all interest in one another. The words she wanted to say kept coming in her throat, yet somehow she knew that she mustn't say them, that the next move must come from him.

She read the paper without realising she was holding it upside down because she was thinking of a usual morning at home. She always got up and took her early cup of tea into her parents' room, curling up on the armchair, discussing the news in the paper with her father while her mother kept yawning and saying: 'Can't we forget politics for one day, John?'

Sheelagh wondered what they were doing now. Missing her? Probably as she was missing them. She felt so uncertain of herself, not sure what to say or if she should speak to Luke about the night before; unsure whether she should keep silent. In the end, Luke made the first move, tossing the paper on the floor.

'You have precisely half an hour to wash, make yourself look beautiful, dress and pack. I have some phoning to do, so I'll see you down at breakfast. In half an hour, mind.'

'All right,' said Sheelagh, glancing at the small travelling clock by her side. 'Aren't we very early?'

'No, the times have been changed,' Luke said, going quickly to the bathroom. She heard the buzzing of his electric razor and hastily jumped out of bed, put on her dressing-gown, collected and folded her clothes to pack them. It looked as if Luke was a punctuality perfectionist like her father. One blessing was that she had been trained well, so at least that would not annoy Luke.

It seemed funny to be already worrying about annoying him. Somehow she had never imagined Luke losing his temper ... at least, not until that hateful woman had phoned about the wedding. If only ... Sheelagh thought, and her eyes stung with unshed tears just as Luke came in. He didn't look at her, but put his clothes in his open suitcase, closed it, locked it and straightened, still not looking at her.

'Leave your luggage here. One of the porters will get it. See you in...' he glanced at his wrist watch, 'fifteen minutes. Right?'

'Right,' she said, but he didn't even wait for her reply but walked with his usual speed out of the room, closing the door behind him.

Fifteen minutes wasn't much, Sheelagh thought rather rebelliously, as she hastily washed, made up and dressed. Yet just the same she was as quick as she could be and walked into the restaurant at exactly the right time.

Luke was waiting, frowning as he looked at his watch. He glanced up and the first smile she had seen on his face since the whole horrible business began lightened his features.

'Good girl,' he said. 'I've ordered breakfast, so we won't have to wait for long.'

Sitting side by side, Sheelagh silently noted that once again he had ordered her food without troubling to ask her what she liked. When it came, it so happened that scrambled eggs with bacon was her favourite meal, but how did he come to know that?

Luke had an uncanny habit of reading her thoughts, for as the waiter brought coffee, he looked at her. 'Nanny told me you preferred scrambled eggs.'

'I do,' Sheelagh agreed, finding it difficult

to speak. Luke was a mass of contradictions, she just couldn't understand him. How could he have been so cruel the night before yet the same man had taken the trouble to learn the kind of food she liked?

They ate quickly and the white Mercedes was waiting for them outside the hotel, but this time with a chauffeur in dark green uniform who smiled at them as he opened the car door.

The drive to the airport was also silent. There was so much she wanted to say, yet this was far from the right place to say it. At the airport, Luke told her to go and sit down and wait for him. He gave her some money and told her what paper and magazines to buy. Again she was startled, for he knew the names of the ones she always read.

She did the shopping and bought herself some pastilles to suck, because though she had flown before, she was always a little nervous. As she sat there, she looked up and saw Luke beckoning her impatiently. Clutching the papers and magazines, she made her way through the crowds of passengers to his side. He had her passport, and tickets, and led the way. Following, she thought that maybe in Italy with all its beauty it might be easier for her to talk to him.

She heard the voice over the Tannoy, but it was hard to hear what was said. This must be the right plane, she thought, for Luke would not make a mistake, so why worry?

Finally Luke handed over their boarding tickets, and took the papers and magazines from her, letting her go up the steps to the plane first. The stewardess in the doorway welcomed them with a smile and greeted Luke by name. Sheelagh found this rather puzzling and then realised that air stewardesses might be on any plane at all at some time or other, so that was how she knew Luke.

They were shown to their seats – first class, Sheelagh realised, and looked quickly at Luke. It must have cost the earth. Could he really afford it? That was another thing, she knew so little about his work, or about his earnings. Her father had asked her questions, but she had said what did it matter, and later her father had admitted that he was satisfied that his daughter would be kept by Luke in *the style to which she was accustomed!* They had ended up by laughing and she had thought no more of it, but now she began to wonder.

The seats were comfortable. Luke began to read a newspaper and she idly turned through the pages of the magazine she had bought. The usual high-pitched sound as the plane cavorted its way round to the take-off came and Luke lowered his paper, telling her to do up her belt. He spoke impatiently and her cheeks were hot as she hastily obeyed. Why had she forgotten it? she wondered.

In an incredibly short time they were high above the clouds and Luke was reading intently. Sheelagh tried to follow his example, but the words seemed to go into circles and didn't make sense. Suddenly the silence was more than she could stand.

'Luke,' she began softly. Not that there were many passengers in the first class part, but at the same time there might be curious ears.

He lowered his paper and turned to look at her. As she had felt before, there was a stranger by her side. This wasn't the Luke she had loved, the Luke she had married. Something had happened.

'Luke.' She moistened her lips with her tongue. No, she couldn't tell him how sorry she was, that it was all her fault and that she loved him. She could not say *that* while he looked at her with those cold eyes.

'When ... when are we landing in Rome?' she asked.

He looked amused, half turning in his seat. 'We're not landing at Rome at all.'

'But I thought...' Her hand flew to her mouth. Had she made a bloomer again? She hated it when he looked at her with that amused contemptuous smile.

'We *were* landing in Rome,' he said slowly, emphasizing the word *were*. 'But I changed my mind.'

'You did? Why?' She couldn't believe it. They had spent so long discussing where they should go, Luke going to a lot of trouble to find out the places she really wanted to see. 'Where are we going, then?'

'We're flying to Blantyre. From Blantyre, we fly to Grande Comoro! It doesn't take long and we may have a few days there before we go on to the island where we're going to live.'

Her eyes were wide with shock. 'But I thought we were going to live in England!'

'I thought so, too, but I've changed my mind.' He picked up the paper. 'You can write and tell your father, because we have a good air mail service. If he's worried, he can come out to make certain I'm looking after you.'

Suddenly Sheelagh was nearly in tears. Everything was turning out so differently from what she had expected and they had planned.

'But, Luke, I thought we were on our honeymoon!'

His face might have been carved out of stone as he looked at her. 'So did I – until last night. One day maybe we'll go on our honeymoon – when, that is, you've got some sense in your little head. So long as ours is a marriage in name only, I prefer to go back to work.'

Sheelagh clutched his arm, holding it tightly, her face quivering.

'But, Luke, I didn't mean...' she began, but even as she spoke, the stewardess was by their side, bringing them glasses of the drinks Luke had asked for. Brandy he had chosen for Sheelagh; so obviously he had found out she was not a good sailor or really happy in the air.

As Sheelagh took the glass and sipped slowly, closing her eyes to keep back the tears, she wondered how any man could be such a mass of contradictions. So cruel and yet so thoughtful. Would she ever understand him? she wondered. Would their marriage ever be a real one?

What would her father say? How anxious he would be, how worried if she wrote and said it was all Luke's doing. Maybe she should say they had decided they would prefer to spend the time in their new home ... maybe she should let her father think that this was what she wanted to do.

Would he believe her? she wondered. She had never been a good liar, yet she didn't want him to come pounding out furiously, for it would only make everything worse where Luke was concerned.

The Comoro Archipelago. How was it she had never heard of them? Luke had admitted they were primitive. This was the place he had taken Georgina to live in and that had made her stop laughing and leave him in six months, the place that the horrible woman had said had killed Georgina. Sheelagh shivered. Surely it was an exaggeration. An island in the Indian Ocean must be beautiful; sunny, with lovely flowers. She glanced at the man by her side, her husband in name only, as he kept throwing at her. He was engrossed in the article he was reading, frowning a little but completely indifferent to the bride by his side.

Suddenly she was swept with a terrible feeling of desolate loneliness. Never before had she felt like this – so utterly alone, so defenceless, so frightened about the future.

She still loved Luke, she would always love him. That wasn't what worried her.

What did was the fear that was growing stronger every moment: would he ever love her again?

CHAPTER 3

Luke hardly spoke during the whole flight out to Blantyre. He must have read every word of the papers and his magazines. Sheelagh pretended to do the same, but she could not have told anyone a single thing about *what* she had read. She felt lost, unable to cope with the situation. Never had she found herself in such a position. Luke had been so different; firm, perhaps, but never unkind or bad-tempered. It was as if he had completely changed. Something had happened between them. Could it be that he still loved Georgina and hated Sheelagh for having reminded him of his first wife?

At Blantyre, he was more friendly, enquiring how she felt, looking after her in his usual protective way, but it still wasn't the same. Walking beside him over the macadam, feeling the hot air blast against her face, the sunshine temporarily blinding her, she was glad of his hand on her arm, yet there was an impersonality about the way his fingers touched her, that frightened her still more. Before, when he held her arm, he had pretended to play a little tune on her bare flesh, smiling down at her, but that day, his fingers were still and he looked straight ahead of him and certainly not down at her.

They went into the second plane that was waiting for them.

'We'll be there soon,' said Luke.

Sheelagh looked up. 'Where are we going?'

He frowned. 'I told you – the Comoro Archipelago Islands. You must have heard of them, surely?'

'I'm afraid geography wasn't my good point.'

'Obviously. Well, it was under the rule of the Arab Sultans when it was first visited by seafaring people from Europe during the sixteenth century. That seems to be the first time they heard of it. The Arabs had introduced their way of life to the natives, and then at a later date it became a French Protected Territory, but now it's independent. Oddly enough it's been overlooked for centuries, but today, people are beginning

59

to see its potentialities.'

'Is that where you live?' she asked a little nervously, for he seemed to jump on her no matter what she said.

'That's where *we* shall live,' he said.

'I know. I mean...' Sheelagh began, suddenly confused because of the way he was looking at her, his eyes narrowed, his mouth a thin line. 'Are there ... are there lots of islands?'

'Quite a few. There may even be more than have been found. Grande Comoro is the largest, the others are – let's see ... Anjouan, Moheli, Dzaoudzi and Nayotte. Our island is called Maloudia, which is a local word that describes waves racing in and pounding against a rocky shore.' He gave an odd little laugh. 'My word, they do, too! The wind that pummels us at times, the great waves that come sweeping in...'

'It sounds rather romantic,' Sheelagh ventured, and saw by his frown that again she had said the wrong thing.

'For heaven's sake, don't you start that line!' he almost snarled. 'There's nothing the least bit romantic about it. A lonely island, still showing the results of the many eruptions the volcanoes have given, the miles of rocky land on which nothing grows.

Primitive is the word.'

'It ... it sounds unusual.'

He gave a grunting little laugh. 'It's that all right. I love it. Just the kind of place that suits me.' He picked up a paper and took out a pen. 'Don't talk while I do this crossword, Sheelagh.'

'I won't,' she promised, her voice thickening as she turned to look out of the window. The plane wasn't very high up and the land below looked like a map spread before them. Her eyes smarted. Why had he to be like that? And what had made him? Surely...?

Although it took only a short time, the journey seemed to her never-ending. She longed to arrive and face up to what lay ahead of her, but just as much she wished she could jump on the next plane and fly back to her home and the loving security she had known. Her father might get impatient at times, but never did he lose his temper. She wasn't used to this kind of tension; this hesitation to open her mouth in case she said the wrong things.

At last the plane began to go down. Sheelagh tried to look relaxed, but closed her eyes tightly, for they went down rather steeply and the earth seemed to come rushing up towards them. Suddenly she shivered, for she felt the warmth of Luke's fingers as they closed round her arm, and played a little tattoo. She looked up quickly and he smiled reassuringly at her.

'It's all right,' he said softly.

'I know, but...' She caught her breath as the plane bounced a little.

'You'll get used to it,' he promised, and in a few moments they were racing across the macadamised strip, hardly bouncing at all.

As she walked down the steps, the heat came to greet her. But it was a different kind of heat from that at Blantyre. This was a scented heat.

'What a lovely smell,' she said impulsively to the tall man by her side.

'Yes. Some people call these islands the Perfume Isles because we grow flowers called ylang-ylang and these flowers are used as a base in the manufacture of perfumes.'

'It's lovely!'

They were soon through the few formalities and Sheelagh saw that quite a number of people were hurrying to a waiting bus, but Luke led the way to a long dark red car. A chauffeur stood waiting, his dark face lighting with his smile as he greeted M'sieur.

Sheelagh yawned and tried to hide it, but Luke had seen.

'Flying can be quite tiring when you're not used to it,' he said as they got into the car. 'An early night is a good idea.'

She looked at him quickly, hopefully. Had he forgiven her? she wondered. The hope was soon to be destroyed, but now as they drove through the streets she noticed vaguely the strange contradictions. On one side might be tall modern glass-fronted office buildings and opposite a large mosque. It was early evening and they saw a crowd of evening worshippers coming out of one elaborately sculpted white mosque, their dark faces above flowing white khanzus, and the veiled women in black who hurried along, almost scuttling as if afraid of being seen. The flat-roofed houses built of grey stone seemed, too, to be huddled together.

They stopped outside a single-storied, rambling hotel that didn't look very much from outside but whose reception hall was luxurious.

Luke strode ahead and Sheelagh followed close behind. He was speaking to the pretty dark-haired girl behind the counter and she was laughing up at him, her eyes mischievous.

'Thanks,' he said, taking the key. 'Try and get those calls through for me, Céleste.

Come, Sheelagh,' he added, taking her arm and almost hustling her down a winding corridor that seemed to go the length of the building.

He unlocked a door and led the way inside. It was a small sitting-room with pale pink curtains, white walls and black carpet, two armchairs and a desk with a small chair. He didn't look round but walked through it to the two doors and opened each. Sheelagh saw, even as she followed him, that the rooms were single. Two single rooms!

'Don't wait up for me, Sheelagh,' Luke said almost curtly. 'I've business to do. I've arranged for dinner to be brought in soon so that you can get some sleep. Goodnight,' he added, and then he was gone, without even a kiss.

Sheelagh stood very still, her hands to her face, her eyes closed. It was worse, if anything. What could she do? What should she do? And suddenly her cheeks flamed painfully as she remembered the receptionist's amusement. She must know they were on their honeymoon, yet Luke had booked two rooms!

Her dinner arrived, delectable sea-food which she enjoyed, followed by a chocolate mousse and then coffee. When the waiter, a tall dark man with a little red fez on his head and wearing an immaculately white suit, took the tray away, there was a terrible stillness. The suite was far down the corridor, close to the end and nowhere near the restaurant or noisy bar. The quietness seemed to enfold her in a frightening way. Was this how her life was going to be in future? she wondered. Would Luke dump her at some place and then vanish for an indefinite period, giving her no idea where or why he went?

However, if that was the way he wanted it, what could she do? At least, at the moment. She showered in the small bathroom and went to bed. She read, or rather pretended to read, her body tense, her ears alert to hear him come in. Deliberately she left her bedroom door open so that she could hear him and welcome him – or perhaps he would see her and stride across the room to take her in his arms, as he had always done before ... before the wedding.

Before that horrible beastly woman. The tears began to come and Sheelagh thrust them away angrily. No good crying, nor was it any good blaming that Viola woman. The fault, Sheelagh decided, lay in herself. She should not have asked Luke about his first wife. No doubt in time he would have told her himself. In any case, did it really matter that he had been married before – or was it her jealousy that had caused the problem – for let's face it, she told herself angrily, she was jealous of that Georgina, who wasn't pretty but always laughed, and she had the uncomfortable feeling that Luke still loved Georgina, even though he might deny it. Never, Sheelagh knew, would she forget the tone of his voice when he said simply: 'Georgina died.' He loved her still. He would never forget her...

Sheelagh buried her face in the pillow. The heat was terrible. She knew there was air-conditioning in the room but had no idea how to switch it on. Instead she let the tears come and they rolled down her cheeks as she hugged the pillow, wishing with all her heart that it was her father she was hugging and that his deep reassuring voice would say: 'Not to worry, darling, we'll sort it out.'

Sheelagh awoke suddenly. The heat had gone and the room was pleasantly cool. By her bedside, was a tray with hot water in a thermos and coffee and milk waiting. She saw, as she slowly came to notice things, that the door she had left open was closed. Luke must have come back, found her asleep, switched on the air-conditioning and closed the door!

She scrambled out of bed, almost tumbling in her haste, as she hurried into the lounge and stopped dead. The door to Luke's room was open, the bed empty, made. Perhaps he hadn't slept in it at all.

Back by her bed, she looked at the clock and stared in amazement. It was half-past eleven. Never before had she slept so long.

After a quick shower she dressed, not wanting to unpack until she knew just how long they were staying at the hotel, for this wasn't where they were going to live; that was on a different, much more primitive island. Funny how frequently Luke said the word *primitive*, almost as if he was trying to frighten her. Or was she wrong and he was merely warning her, not wanting her to expect too much and therefore be disappointed? As Georgina, his first wife, had been.

Dressed, Sheelagh brushed back her hair, thinking that maybe she would have it cut short, for long hair could be uncomfortably hot in a tropical climate. Slowly she walked down the long corridor and was glad to see that Céleste was not behind the counter but an elderly man.

'Ah, Madame Jessop,' he greeted her with

a smile. 'We are delighted to meet you. You are better, I trust? Your husband said you were not well on the plane.'

'I'm much better, thank you,' Sheelagh said, and smiled. Then she spoke in French. 'I think I would like to see the town.'

The elderly man's face broke in a smile. He replied in French. 'Madame has a beautiful accent. I am happy that you should speak my language. You wish to walk? Certainly, Madame, but we cannot let you walk alone. If you will wait...' He pushed the bell by his side and Sheelagh waited, a little annoyed, for she wanted no companion, also rather worried in case it might turn out to be Céleste!

But it wasn't. It was a plump middle-aged woman with red cheeks, dark eyes to match her hair and a friendly smile. She also spoke French. She wore a very thin white frock, almost reaching the ground, and had a wisp of veil on her head.

'I shall be only too happy to show Madame Jessop round,' she said with a little mixture of a bow and a curtsey which startled Sheelagh. 'We think a great deal of your husband, Madame. You are a very fortunate lady,' she said in French. 'We walk slowly. The heat is great.'

How right she was, Sheelagh thought, as

they walked down the streets. Madame Bordin talked eagerly, delighted in the chance to show the beauty of the town. It was indeed a strange mixture of modernity and the past. They paused to admire the beautiful carved wooden doors, the tiny shops with dark insides but brightened by the rolls of vividly coloured cloth. The many mosques, some small, some enormous with beautifully sculptured decorations. They paused at the market place, vivid with the most beautiful orchids Sheelagh had ever seen, but walked hurriedly by the stalls where raw meat was displayed and left them with no desire to stay! The huge offices were a contrast with the one-storey houses with their flat roofs. Everything was colourful. A surprising amount of traffic, many different kinds of people, in dresses of their own nationality.

As if Madame Bordin guessed her thoughts, 'On this island,' she said in French, 'we have had so many masters and so many fathers. We are a mixed lot.' She shrugged. *'C'est la vie,'* she added philosophically.

Sheelagh was quite glad when she saw the hotel ahead of her, for she found the hot air tiring and was already fighting the desire to yawn.

'It was good of you to go with me, Madame,' she said.

The middle-aged woman beamed. 'It was an honour to me to escort Monsieur Jessop's wife. We are happy that he has married again.'

'You...' Sheelagh hesitated. Should she ask questions or would Luke take offence and call it *snooping?* She decided to risk it. 'You knew the first Mrs Jessop?' she asked in English, without realising she had changed her language.

Madame Bordin looked puzzled. 'We know her? It is not so. My husband and I, we were not here in those days. It must be...' She frowned thoughtfully, her lips moving silently as if she was counting the years. 'It must be about eleven years ago. We were in Madagascar then. My husband, he was working there. Then he retired and we came here,' she said in French.

They had reached the hotel. Again Sheelagh thanked her and quickly escaped down the corridor to the coolness of her room, there to fling off her damp clothes and stand under the shower. She felt absurdly sleepy, and could not understand it.

She had just finished dressing when she heard a man cough. The hairbrush stayed poised in the air, her arm going still. Luke was back!

Hastily looking in the mirror, straightening her pale pink dress, patting her hair, she hurriedly opened the door to the sitting-room.

'Luke!' she began eagerly, then stopped dead, shocked with surprise, for the man who was sitting in the armchair, reading a newspaper, lowered it and looked up – and he wasn't Luke.

He was the ugliest, most frightening-looking man she had ever seen. Absurdly, though it wasn't funny, he looked like Humpty Dumpty, for he had a terrifically high forehead and not a wisp of hair on his head, a long pale face with no moustache and not a hair on his upper lip or chin. Slowly he rose, reminding her of the movements of a turtle. Relentless, slow but determined.

'Who are you?' she gasped. And then she remembered what Luke had said. 'Mercury!' she said, her hand going to her mouth. 'I'm afraid I don't know your surname.'

He came slowly to meet her and she had to fight the impulse to turn and run, slam the bedroom door, turning the key, putting the furniture against it. Never had she been so frightened. He was a big fat man, as round as he was tall. Luckily he was *not* tall, being only a few inches taller than Sheelagh.

'Welcome to the Islands, my dear Sheelagh,' he said. His voice startled her still more, for it was soft, gentle, almost apologetic, completely different from his appearance.

He held out his hand – a huge white hand that made her shudder, but somehow she found the courage to put her hand in his, half dreading the crush he would surely give it, again surprised because of the gentle grip he gave it and then instantly let go.

'Please sit down. I would like us to have a little talk,' he said.

'I'm afraid Luke isn't in–' Sheelagh hesitated as she watched him make his slow progress back to his chair.

'I know. That's why I am here.' He waved to the other chair. 'Please sit down, Sheelagh,' he said, his voice still gentle, but this time she heard a steely note in it. This was a man accustomed to being obeyed. After all, he was Luke's boss ... or was he? If only she knew more about Luke, she thought unhappily, as she sat down, folded her hands and looked at him.

'You are feeling better, Sheelagh?' he asked.

'I was only tired. I...'

'Still am? I am not surprised. I loathe flying, but when time is so expensive one has no choice. Always, afterwards, it takes me days before I am my proper self. This I think you will find. It won't be so hot on your island.' He paused as if waiting for a question, but Sheelagh said nothing. She felt on edge, wary in case she should say the wrong thing and make things worse with Luke.

'So?' Mercury sounded amused. 'You are Luke's second wife. You are very much prettier, but also much younger. I was surprised when Luke told me your age. Man, I said, have some sense. She is barely out of the cradle and you are approaching middle age. But he would not listen.' Mercury gave another chuckle. 'Love is a strange thing.' Suddenly he frowned, his voice growing harsh. 'I trust you will make a better wife than his last one did.'

Again, another silence. Sheelagh's hands were moist with heat, her head throbbing. She sensed the animosity in the man's eyes as he glared at her and waited.

Somehow she found her voice. 'I shall do my best,' she said, then thought how corny it sounded.

'It won't be easy,' he told her, and sounded pleased that he could say it. 'Life married to a man like Luke could never be easy. I still think that men like us should remain bachelors. No,' he added with a strange smile, 'you are right. I can see what you are thinking. I was a fool, too. I married. Marriage isn't easy, you know.'

'I know,' she said, then wished she hadn't as she saw the amusement in his eyes. Had she given it away? Would he tell Luke what she had said? she wondered. 'My parents told me that,' she added quickly.

'Ah. You miss your parents?' Mercury asked. 'Already?'

'I... No, I don't miss them,' Sheelagh said at once. In a way it was true, in another, it wasn't, for she wished that her father could walk into the room and get rid of this hateful man.

'Perhaps you will be different from Georgina,' Mercury said. 'She had no brains. All she wanted was money – more and more money. In those days, Luke had little. Today he has plenty. Was that why you married him?'

It was the final straw. Sheelagh found herself on her feet, completely unaware how beautiful she looked with her cheeks suddenly red, her eyes blazing with anger. 'I most certainly did not marry Luke for his money!' She flung the words at the fat man. 'I wouldn't mind if he ... if he was ... was a ... pauper!' At last she found the word she wanted. 'I...'

The door leading to the corridor opened and Luke stood there. The words died away as Sheelagh stared at him, waiting for his sarcasm, perhaps his anger with her for having shouted at his employer.

Instead he smiled. 'So you two have met. Good. I came along to see how you were, Sheelagh. Feeling better?'

She looked at him and thought of all that she wanted to say and couldn't – at least not at that moment.

'I'm afraid I still feel sleepy,' she confessed.

Mercury heaved himself to his feet, panting as he spoke. 'I told her it might last for a few days. You're on time, Luke.' He glanced at the huge gold watch on his wrist. 'Come along, the conference is due to start in ten minutes.' He turned and bowed, rather dramatically, which Sheelagh took as a jibe. 'I am sorry I must take your husband from you so much, but you have many years ahead.' He cackled with laughter as he made his slow ponderous way to the door.

'You're going again, Luke?' Sheelagh

couldn't stop from saying.

He gave her a curious look. 'It's better this way. Have an early night again,' he said, and this time he kissed her, lightly on the cheek. Mercury turned at that moment and chuckled. Sheelagh wondered if Luke had kissed her to keep Mercury from knowing they had quarrelled. And then the door was shut and she was alone again.

A knock came and the waiter wheeled in a trolley with her late lunch. Again she enjoyed the seafood and after she had drunk her coffee, went to lie on her bed. She felt strangely lethargic, as if everything was an effort. Yet she had to make an effort to tell Luke how sorry she was and to stop this dreadful coldness, because it could only get worse. If she wasn't to lose his love altogether, she must do something about it soon.

She awoke to a still empty suite. Later she showered and dressed, for surely he would come and have dinner with her?

He did, but he was in such a hurry that it made things even worse. He came in, showered, vanished into his room, came out glancing at his wrist watch.

'We've got just half an hour and then I must be off,' he said. 'Mercury wants me to meet someone of importance.'

'Luke, I must talk to you,' said Sheelagh, almost desperately, clutching his sleeve. 'Who is this Mercury? Your boss?'

Luke lifted her hand and removed it from his arm. He did it gently, but the movement shocked and hurt her so much, she could hardly bear it.

'He's my partner. He was once my boss. Actually, he liked you.'

'He liked me?' Sheelagh's voice was bitter. 'You mean he hated me. He was just as nasty as he could be, and he looks positively revolting!'

'That's not his fault – it's glandular trouble. He's got an odd way. You'll get used to it.'

'He said nasty things about marriage.'

Luke laughed. 'He always does. Says that to every bride. Actually he was pleased with you. You lost your temper.'

'I'm sorry.' Sheelagh spread out her hands in a helpless gesture. 'He accused me of marrying you for your money.'

'Don't be sorry. He was delighted. It isn't many people who aren't scared of him. He likes someone with guts.'

'What's his name?'

'Mercury. Oh, his surname? His real name is James William Potter, but he hates the name as he hated his family and when he was a youngster he was interested in chemistry and got into some sort of trouble with mercury. I don't know the details, he'll never tell them, but he got the nickname of Mercury and it's stuck. He'll be really annoyed should you call him Mr Potter.'

'And I mustn't annoy him?' Sheelagh stared at Luke.

He stared back. For a moment they stood, close yet not touching one another at all. It was as if they were suspended in space, each waiting for the other to move.

Luke moved first, glancing at his watch. 'Hell, I'm starving, so we'd better go and eat.'

'Luke, please, just one minute.' Sheelagh didn't clutch his arm this time, she was too afraid of another brush-off. 'We must talk. I want to tell you...'

His face changed. 'This is no place for talking. It can wait until we get home.'

'But when will we be home?'

'Maybe tomorrow, maybe next week. It depends.'

'On Mercury, I suppose.'

He frowned. 'Don't be absurd. We'd better go and eat.'

He opened the door and she had to almost

run to keep up with his long effortless strides. They hardly talked through dinner. Normally Sheelagh would have enjoyed the meal, for it was the kind of food she loved, but Luke's silence hurt her terribly and his refusal to listen to her made it worse.

He left her immediately after dinner. 'Don't wait up,' he said curtly as he bent to kiss her cheek lightly. These kisses, she felt, made it far worse than if he hadn't kissed her at all, for there was no emotion in them, they were just a gesture for any onlooker who might glance their way. That seemed strange to her, too, for Luke wasn't the kind of man to worry about what people said or thought of him, so why should he worry?

Unless, she thought as she walked slowly back down the corridor to her room, he was sensitive about it, thinking that everyone knew his first marriage had been a failure, and was afraid they might know that this one was, too.

A failure? The words cut into her like a sharp knife. Whatever happened, it mustn't be a failure.

She undressed, wearing her pink nightie and her transparent negligée, then she went into Luke's bedroom and curled up in his armchair. She was afraid to lie on his bed in case she slept and she must stay awake so that as soon as he came in, she could rush into his arms and tell him how sorry she was, and she didn't mind if he had a hundred wives so long as he loved her.

Something must have awakened her, for as she opened her eyes, she felt stiff, looking wonderingly round the room. Why was she in an armchair? Slowly consciousness took the place of sleepiness and she remembered she was in Luke's bedroom. And his bed was empty.

She looked at the watch on her wrist. It was five o'clock! She had slept all night and Luke was still not back. Yawning, stretching, she went back to her own room and stopped in the doorway. Luke was in her bed, sprawled under the crumpled sheet, his face relaxed in sleep.

Standing close to him, she looked down, longing to stroke his face, to let her cheek touch his, her arms round his neck, yet afraid that by doing so, she might make everything worse.

At that moment, he opened his eyes. 'What the...' he began, and sat up, the sheet falling away from his naked chest. 'Oh, it's you,' he said, looking at her then grabbed his dressing-gown and leapt out of bed.

'Look at the time! I told Mercury I'd be there at four o'clock as we've some crates to get dispatched. Sheelagh, we're going home this morning. I'll be round to fetch you at ten o'clock, so have everything packed, see?' Tying his belt round his waist, he walked past her as if she didn't exist, going into the bathroom and turning on the shower.

She gave up! It was just impossible to talk to Luke. She felt she didn't want to go to sleep again. Ten o'clock she must be ready. Meanwhile?

She heard the other door of the bathroom slam and knew Luke was in his own room. She sat on the edge of her bed, touching the pillow where his head had lain and stifling a sigh. Maybe he was right, maybe it was better to wait until they were at home. How odd, yet how lovely those words sounded. *At home. Their home.*

Surely there they could find a way of putting things right? They simply had to, she thought, feeling the urgency go through her. She loved him. Somehow or other she must find a way to convince him that she did.

At ten minutes to ten, Sheelagh was ready. Everything was packed. She was wearing a clean thin blue sheath dress, her hair tied back. She sat by the small table, re-reading the letter she had written to her father.

It had been a difficult letter to write. Indeed, she had begun it three times and torn up what she had written. Even this she wasn't sure about. Her father was no fool, he knew her well. Would the bunch of lies she had written seem to him feasible?

Reading it slowly, she nodded her head as she agreed with what she had written. She had said that *owing to circumstances beyond their control* – at least, Sheelagh thought, that would make him laugh, for it was one of their favourite joking excuses when they were late for a meal. Not that her mother ever found it funny, but Sheelagh and her father would roll in their seats with mirth, Sheelagh secretly wondering why her mother had no sense of humour.

Anyhow, there it was. *'Owing to circumstances beyond our control...'* which was true in a way! ... *'we decided we'd postpone our honeymoon.'* Was that true, too? she wondered, but Luke *had* said just that, *'and come out here to our home.'*

That had needed a lot of thinking about, for her father, as she had herself believed or rather had understood, they were going to live in England. Yet, looking back, Sheelagh had to admit that Luke had never said such a thing. As he had been working in England for a year, though he was often away for days at a time, she had taken it for granted his job was there. Yet ... but that was another thing: Luke *had* said *he* had thought he was going to live in England. What had changed that? Was it some of Mercury's maliciousness, thinking he could ruin their marriage this way – or was it because that Viola woman had turned up in Luke's life to his fury – or was it, Sheelagh wondered, *her* fault, because she had certainly angered him by her questions.

Yet were they so wrong? Wouldn't anyone be upset about it? Had she committed such an unforgivable crime? After all, when you love someone, you can expect to know about their past.

Or can you? she asked herself.

Sighing, she read on. 'We are here on the Comoro Islands. Dad, you probably know about them, but I didn't. It seems they grow an amazing flower with the most odd name, hlang or something. No – ylang-ylang, that's it, and this is exported to France for making perfume. It's a fascinating town, all mixed people, and the most beautiful mosques, so white. We're off today to the island where

83

we'll settle down for a time. I'll write and tell you all about it.'

Well, maybe it wasn't so bad, Sheelagh thought as she folded the letter and put it in the envelope, glancing at her watch. If she was quick, she might be able to take it to Monsieur Bordin and ask him to post it airmail for her, as there might be a delay from their island.

She was half way down the corridor when Luke came along.

'Where are you off to?' he asked, and she heard the impatient anger in his voice.

'Just to ... just to post a letter.'

He twisted her round, his hand rough on her shoulder, almost pushing her back to their suite. 'Writing to dear daddy, I suppose. Weeping on his shoulder, telling him what a bully of a husband you have, how he neglects, leaves you alone. Where is it?'

'No, I didn't!' Sheelagh put her hand with the letter in it behind her back, but Luke was too quick for her. He grabbed the letter and held it high above her. 'Give it to me, Luke,' she snapped angrily. 'That's my letter!'

'A husband has the right to read his wife's correspondence,' he said, holding the letter high so that she could not reach it and tearing it open.

84

'You have no such right!' Sheelagh began angrily, for her father would never have dreamt of opening her mother's letters.

Luke's face changed. It seemed to turn to stone.

'You don't need to remind me,' he said. 'I haven't forgotten our marriage is in name only.' He opened the door and looked at the suitcases. 'You're ready?'

'Luke, I didn't mean that!' Sheelagh cried out, clutching his arm. Without turning, he shook her off.

'I doubt if you know what you mean at any time,' he said curtly. 'The porter's coming for the luggage. The car's outside.'

He gave her little time to collect her handbag and she had almost to run to keep up with him. She saw to her dismay, Céleste behind the counter. Céleste was smiling.

'See you soon, I hope, Mr Jessop,' she said gaily, then looked at Sheelagh. 'I hope you're feeling better,' she said, but her eyes were amused. Did she know? Sheelagh wondered, squirming unhappily. Did Mercury know? Did everyone know what a failure their marriage was up to date?

She sat in the back of the long dark red car. The chauffeur greeted her with a friendly smile, but Luke sat silently by her

85

side, ruffling through some papers, frowning as he wrote on the margin of the notes.

They drove along a rather narrow strip of tar once they had left Moroni, past some fishing villages with strange little boats out at sea, each with a fisherman sitting in them. She wondered what the boats were called; they looked more like trunks of trees that had been hollowed out and with balancing arms on either side and a pole stuck at one end, with a lamp hanging on it. She glanced at Luke, but he was frowning, so she decided to say nothing. He still had her father's letter. Would Luke really read it? she wondered, hoping he would and then hoping he wouldn't. It was difficult to know what was best to do, Luke had developed such a strange temper. Indeed, he seemed exactly like a stranger. Were all men like this when they were married? she found herself wondering. Did they put on an act to please their beloved? Yet could they keep it up, if it was unnatural, for a whole year?

Now they had left the villages and on either side of the narrow road was lush tropical vegetation. Hundreds of coconut trees, the palms moving in the slight breeze. Strange bushes and trees, with huge fruits hanging from them. How interested her father would be in it all, she thought. Then suddenly the car turned sharply left, leaving behind the trees and shrubs and taking them towards the blue sea.

It was so beautiful that she had exclaimed, 'How lovely!' before she knew it.

There was a wide cove of white sand, the water peaceful in the small lagoon. Sheltering the quiet water from the huge waves, which were breaking angrily, were the rocks of the corral reef. There was a small jetty and, to Sheelagh it seemed, a very small steamer was anchored waiting.

'Are we going on that?' she asked, again before she stopped to think.

Luke was putting his papers into a briefcase. 'Of course,' he said. 'You'll get used to it.'

She looked at him in dismay. She just couldn't bear it if she was sick. He put his hand in the pocket of his fawn-coloured linen suit and pulled out a flask. Pouring some of the flask's contents into a cardboard cup, he passed it to her.

'Brandy's the best deterrent,' he said, and his voice was kind. It was the voice she knew, the voice she loved. 'We shan't be long, Sheelagh, and it isn't as bad as it looks.'

Wasn't it? she was to wonder later, as she

stood by the rail on the small steamer, and they drew away from the jetty, which was crowded with workmen in white overalls who had been carrying on board the goods that were stacked in the lower decks. Luke had gone off with the captain and she stood alone, looking at the narrow opening to the lagoon, with the huge pointed rocks standing like sentinels on either side. She closed her eyes as they went through the narrow opening, the huge waves racing to meet them, seeming to toss them in the air and then let them come down with a reverberating bang. Her fingers clung tightly to the rail and she opened her eyes slowly. They were out in it now, the great waves pounding the sides of the steamer almost viciously.

'You'll get used to it in time,' a soft voice said – a voice Sheelagh recognised.

Startled and dismayed, she turned. It was Mercury, all right, standing by her side, the short, squarely-fat man with the huge egg-like bald head, the strange eyes that seemed to be squinting but was, she knew, not so, for his left eye was of glass.

'I'm ... I'm not a good sailor,' Sheelagh said, aware that she might betray the fact at any moment and that after all it was nothing to be ashamed of, because it wasn't her fault.

'Few of us are, but we get used to it. Did Luke give you some brandy? I told him to.'

'Yes, he did,' said Sheelagh, her voice suddenly lifeless. So it wasn't Luke who had thought of her, it was Mercury. Luke didn't care, but he carried out Mercury's advice. It hurt ... for she had known a moment of hopefulness when he had produced the flask and she had thought gratefully of his consideration. Instead it was Mercury's consideration, not Luke's!

'You've never been to these islands before?' Mercury asked.

'I've never heard of them,' she confessed.

'Lots of people haven't, but they're beginning to get known. Good tourist potentiality, but at the same time it seems a shame to crowd these beautiful islands with tourists.'

'You get many?'

'Too many, I think, but there, *c'est la vie*. Our island isn't too bad, though. We're concentrating on flowers and minerals at the moment as well as tourists. There's a terrific future there. Your husband has his head screwed on all right.' He chuckled. 'Sometimes screwed on too tightly for my liking. Obstinate, that's what he is – stubborn. He hates being told what to do or asked questions.'

Sheelagh stared at the hideously ugly man and fidgeted unhappily. Had he said those last words on purpose? Was he warning her? Or was he letting her know that Luke had told him about their quarrel?

'Do *you* mind being asked questions?' Mercury demanded.

Sheelagh was startled. The steamer had settled into a deep roll, every now and then being lifted in the air and dropped with a resounding splash. 'I don't think so,' she answered.

'Well, what sort of girl are you?' Mercury asked. 'I mean, girls of your age today are very different from what they were when I was your age. You're permissive, you love the ghastly long-haired vandals, adore terrifically loud pop music that nearly drives me mad and are never satisfied, always asking for more. Strikes me, you're different. What sort of job had you?'

'I didn't have one,' Sheelagh began, then found herself telling him what she had told Luke – how she hadn't been very bright at school except for languages, and when she left her mother had been ill so she automatically nursed her, and then... 'You see, Dad was retired and bored to tears, so we just went places together – playing golf,

gardening, fishing. Name it and we did it.'
She laughed, a happy sound as she thought
back to the days when she had no problems
at all, and, if she had one, her father would
'fix it'. 'We used to go out in the car and just
follow a crazy plan like turn left, then right
twice, then left four times ... and we used to
go along the country lanes and we saw the
most gorgeously beautiful country that way.'

'You enjoyed it?'

'I did, very much,' Sheelagh began, then
hesitated. Had she said too much about her
past happiness? Would he twist her words?

It seemed he was going to do just that.
'You'll find this life very different. I hope
you won't hate it.'

Sheelagh frowned. 'I do wish you and Luke
wouldn't keep implying that I'll hate it. How
can I know until I live there?' Anger swept
through her and her voice rose. 'Why should
I be unhappy? There's always plenty of work
to do in running a house, then I love gardening and you seem to grow the most super
orchids. I'll have plenty to do, I'm sure.'

'Luke is away a lot. You may be lonely,'
said Mercury.

Shrugging her shoulders, Sheelagh
frowned. 'I'll find plenty to do. I've always
wanted to paint, but never had the time.'

'Here you'll have plenty,' he said, and suddenly smiled. 'I see you've got it all planned out.'

'It's better that way,' Sheelagh said, her voice defiant. 'I intend to make Luke a good wife and I shan't be that if I'm unhappy. I don't intend to be unhappy, either,' she finished, her voice rising angrily again.

'Good on you,' Mercury said, his face split by a grin. 'You're the kind of girl I shoulda married!'

Sheelagh thought it was her turn. 'What kinda girl did you marry?' she asked, deliberately copying his voice.

He chuckled. 'A beauty, Sheelagh, a real beauty. Red hair. I've always liked a redhead and I thought if I married one, we'd have the greatest of rows. Redheads are quick-tempered, you know. What a mistake! My wife's the meekest little mouse. When I get mad, her eyes grow huge and scared and I feel an absolute heel. Look,' he grinned again, 'what say you let me come and quarrel with you when I'm feeling bad? Sometimes things get my goat and I'm about to blow up. Then I have a row with the nearest person. Luke and I fight like mad, but somehow it isn't such fun as he's so big and I'm so small.' He chuckled, his eyes twinkling.

Sheelagh found herself chuckling too. The thought of Mercury being *small* was hilarious.

'So as I'm small you think we could fight?' she joked. 'No holds barred?'

'Hi, watch your step, Sheelagh! I'm not committing myself. You girls of today are too bright for one of my age. You can probably toss me over your shoulder without turning a hair and I'd wonder what'd hit me.'

Sheelagh began to laugh, she just could not stop. The suggestion that she could toss the enormous body of Mercury over her shoulder was the funniest thing she had ever heard.

'Okay,' she said. 'We'll quarrel, but we won't fight.'

His face sobered. 'I'd be obliged, but one thing, Sheelagh, if I say things that hurt, remember I don't mean them. I'm just letting off steam. If I don't, I'll explode just as a lidless kettle would, and that's not good for my health.'

'Well, Sheelagh, how goes it?' asked Luke.

Sheelagh turned eagerly, her face brightening. 'Luke!'

Mercury laughed. 'I'll leave you youngsters alone. We'll be there in fifteen minutes,' he said, and walked down the deck, vanishing inside.

'You've been talking to Mercury?'

'Yes. He's a strange man, Luke,' Sheelagh said quickly. 'One moment I hate him, the next he has me in fits of laughter and I can't help liking him.'

'I know. Same with me. His bark can be vicious, but he doesn't mean a word.'

'He's asked me to quarrel with him as his wife won't!'

Luke laughed. 'She's terrified of him, yet she adores him. For all his harshness, that man is the most thoughtful I know. Did you wonder why he came with us today? To see you're settled down all right, because he says a bachelor doesn't bother and he's not having you start on the wrong foot. He talked with you on the trip to keep you from thinking about the rough waves. I bet you forgot them.'

'I did,' she confessed. 'Is that the island ... our island?' she asked, pointing to the distant blur she had vaguely noticed and that seemed to be coming closer every moment.

'Yes, that's Maloudia, our home,' he told her, and for a moment, put his arm round her, his voice changing. 'I hope you'll be happy there, Sheelagh.'

Sheelagh looked up at him and heard the

running of footsteps on the decks as the men came to prepare for the landing.

'We'll be happy, Luke,' she said softly – but so softly that in the sudden noise, she wondered if he heard.

CHAPTER 4

Sheelagh stared at the island which was to be, at any rate temporarily, her home.

From first sight it fascinated her, for somehow it was so different from any island she had seen before.

Ahead was the lagoon they were making for where the entrance through the coral reef was far larger than at Moroni, so the lagoon was not the smooth, wrinkleless sheet of water she had seen before, but one far more disturbed, the small boats rocking wildly. The island itself had a personality all of its own, for above the harbour were two tall rugged mountain peaks looking as if they had been cleft in half by some massive powerfully-handed axe. Down in the hollow crouched a small cluster of single-storied houses, most of them made of grey stone.

On one side was the tall steeple of a church, on the other the dignity of a small but beautiful white mosque. The jetty was crowded, not only with workmen in white shorts and shirts but with women wearing all different kinds of clothes, some in vivid colours, others in dark robes.

As the steamer came closer to the jetty there was a great noise, a mixture of eager voices, shouts, songs and laughter.

Luke was standing silently by her side but a little behind her and she had the uncomfortable feeling that he was watching her face, waiting to see her reaction.

She looked up past the little town. All the island seemed a strange mixture of rising pointed hills, bare rocks, and the slopes to the valleys that were packed with trees. Along the coastline she could see a distant cove where the big waves came racing in to fling themselves at the rocks angrily.

'Well,' said Mercury, coming so quietly to Sheelagh's side that she actually jumped, turning to look at him, 'what do you think of it?'

'I've never seen anything like it,' Sheelagh admitted. 'It seems such a mixture of barrenness and lushness.'

'Just right, my dear,' Mercury sounded

delighted. 'You've put your little finger on it. It is a mixture. That's due to the violent eruptions that took place last century.'

'Is the volcano alive?'

He shook his huge hideous head slowly. 'Not to my knowledge. Just now and then it rumbles and the earth seems to move, but nothing's come of it. Still, it might one day, you know.' His real eye was twinkling as he stared at her, as if expecting her to look afraid.

She smiled instead. 'I'm not biting, Mercury,' she told him.

He let out a roar of laughter, clapped her so hard on the back that she nearly fell forward, and looked at Luke. 'You've got someone here, Luke, my lad. Just my cuppa tea!'

They were alongside the jetty, instantly everyone seemed to be moving. Islanders swarmed aboard as the porters staggered under huge crates and the cranes on the ship slowly waved the heavier items ashore.

A station wagon was waiting. Mercury led the way, waddling slowly, talking over his shoulder to Sheelagh.

'I'm just coming to make sure all's right with the world. This has come about so sudden-like, we've not had time to prepare for you, my dear. My wife'd be shocked to think you'd come without warning, but I'll see to it.'

Inside the car it was very hot. Sheelagh tried not to show that it was affecting her, but her hair felt a mess, tossed about by the wind at sea, and her cheeks burned. Luke was not with them. He was talking to two men, frowning a little while Mercury chattered away.

'There's a real mixture of natives here and most of the language is a sorta mixture. Good thing you talk French, because that'll help. It was under French protection, you know, and many of them still swear they're for the French,' he chuckled.

Luke joined them, sitting behind the wheel and starting the car. They drove down the narrow street with shops on either side – rather sad-looking, dark-windowed shops, Sheelagh thought – and then past the market where she could see piles of different fruits and women and children selling them. The road went through the cleft between the two enormous pointed rocks and began to climb. It was a circular climb gradually going up the mountain behind the cleft rocks. It was indeed strange, for part of the mountain was covered with big trees, massed together, and another part would be covered with black-looking, dried-up liquid with not a green thing, leaf or bush, in sight.

After about half an hour they came to more flat land that was near the ocean.

'We're t'other side of the island now,' Mercury, breathing heavily by Sheelagh's side, explained. 'This is the tourists' side, so to speak.' She could see the long stretches of white sand, the waves outside the reefs, the palm trees moving slightly in the breeze. 'This is the hotel we've built,' Mercury went on. 'We won't stop now as we've business to do, but it's not bad. See?'

Sheelagh nodded, looking interestedly at the row of thatched-roofed small chalets, each with a little balcony. A paved pathway joined them all and led to a larger building that seemed made like the outside lines of the letter E. In the centre was a large stretch of grass with tables and brightly coloured sunshades over each. There were people sitting in chairs, some in the sun, others lying on the white sand which was on the other side of the narrow road.

'We took you this way to show you the hotel,' Mercury explained. 'Normally there's a higher road. Not that we get much traffic.' He chuckled, his laughter rumbling from inside him. 'Thanks be!'

They came to a small lagoon and there were people swimming in it. 'That's what most of 'em do,' Mercury said. 'Really tickles me, that does. Spend all this money just to lie in the sun or swim. Why don't they stay at home and do it?' He looked at her shrewdly. 'You sit in the sun much?'

Sheelagh laughed. 'When there is any sun!'

'You'll get plenty here. You've come at a good time. April to October is our best, because there's little rain and the heat's not too great.'

The car was climbing again, going circularly round another bleak mountain and then abruptly going down a steep incline. Again they were close to the ocean, but, above the road, a plateau jutted out and on it was a large white two-storied house.

'That's mine,' Mercury said proudly as they drove by underneath, Sheelagh having to lean out of the window to look up at the house. 'My wife doesn't like it. She's scared it might fall.' He laughed scornfully. 'It could never do that.'

Sheelagh sympathised with Mercury's wife, because it looked horribly precarious, balanced above the road.

'You and Luke must come to dinner one

night. Can't be today as I'm going back soon as I've got you settled in,' Mercury went on. 'Ah, there are the flowers we were talking about.' He pointed to a long, apparently endless field full of small yellow flowers. 'Slow up a bit, Luke, my boy.'

Luke obeyed. Sheelagh looked at the flowers, puzzled, for they were such funny-looking ones – small, yellow, with this delicious fragrance that swept into the car, yet they weren't like ordinary flowers, for they grew out of stunted trees.

'Deliberately stunted, those trees,' Mercury told her. 'We do a good trade here.'

Luke accelerated and they sped through the field of yellow flowers, then turned inland again, climbing once more. Sheelagh began to wonder where their house was, and would she have to go all the way back to that little town to do their shopping? Once again the road began to drop, this time into a deep valley where they were surrounded by tall trees, which were crowded together, tall, slender trees, reaching up into the sky as if thirsty. After some time in this rather eerie valley, for there was little light only what filtered down through the leaves, they came into an open space. It was above sea level, also on a plateau but this time without a deep drop below. On it was a single-storied house with thatched roof and a long wide verandah in front of it. There were a few big pots of flowers, vividly crimson, but the garden looked sorely neglected.

'T'ch, Luke, you've let it go,' said Mercury, his voice critical. 'Looks really scruffy. You good at gardening, Sheelagh?'

'Not good, because I've never done it alone, but I always helped Dad.'

She saw Luke's shoulders move a little and wondered why.

The car was slowing up at the side of the house.

'You drive?' Mercury asked.

'Yes, Dad taught me, but...' She saw the frown on Luke's face as he parked the car and turned. Was it the word *dad* that angered him? she wondered.

Mercury grinned. 'Done much driving?'

'Not much, you see...' She stopped dead, her puzzled eyes watching Luke's cold face. 'You see ... you see he didn't like being driven by anyone.'

Mercury chuckled. 'Don't blame him. Used to feel that way myself, but these days, somehow my body and the steering wheel don't get on comfortably.'

Sheelagh couldn't help laughing as she

looked at him. She wondered if any car was big enough to get that enormous stomach behind the steering wheel.

'Got the girl a car, Luke?' Mercury asked.

'Not yet,' Luke almost snapped. 'Give me time, man.'

'Of course, son. Only think she's going to be kinda lonely here without transport.'

'I'll see to it,' Luke snapped. 'Well, here we are, Sheelagh. At home.'

She looked at the house, and wondered what her father would have called it. A shack? She got out of the car, went towards the steps, glancing at the screen-covered door, but Mercury's hand was on her arm.

'Steady on, Sheelagh. Don't jump your fences. Come on, Luke,' Mercury chuckled. 'A bridegroom has to carry his bride over the doorstep. You're lucky she's so small. Shoulda seen me striving to carry my Diane over, me so small and she so tall. Wait till you see my wife, Sheelagh. She's a real beauty!'

Sheelagh stood very still, almost afraid to breathe. How was Luke going to react? she wondered. There was nothing she would like more than to be carried over the threshold by him. But how did he feel about it?

She was not left long to wonder, for almost

as Mercury spoke, Luke picked her up, carrying her effortlessly in his arms as he kicked the door open and climbed up the stairs to the long screen-surrounded verandah.

Sheelagh closed her eyes, loving the feel of his arms round her. If only they were alone, she could have put her arms round his neck, her cheek against his, her mouth close as she whispered:

'I'm so sorry, Luke darling. I don't mind if you've been married a hundred times, but just forgive me. I love you so.'

But she couldn't do it with Mercury chuckling there, making jokes.

Luke put her down gently and she felt a chill as his arms let go of her. She looked down the long wide verandah, saw the deep armchairs, covered with a hideous blue material. Mercury had shambled ahead, Luke behind. She could hear Mercury complaining.

'Never seen such dirt! I know they didn't expect you. All the same, why the ... do we pay 'em if they don't work? Where's that girl? Tarantula! Tarantula!' he bellowed.

Sheelagh suddenly felt tired. She sat down in one of the chairs, letting her head go back, closing her eyes. This was all so very different from what she had dreamed.

Not that Luke could be blamed at all. As he had said, he had not expected to come out now, so he had given the staff no warning. If only they could be alone ... if only Mercury would go!

Suddenly the two men were towering above her.

'Not to worry, Sheelagh,' said Mercury. 'You're tired, and I'm not surprised. Tarantula's bringing you something to eat. Luke and I have got to go off now, but he'll be back later. The girl will clean up the place, so I'd stay where you are for the time being. See you one day soon. Coming, Luke?' He turned to the silent man by his side and then turned back. 'I nearly forgot. Look, Sheelagh, you say you're good at French? I wonder if you'd help me. I got hold of some manuscripts written several centuries ago about this island. Might be interesting, maybe helpful. I keep meaning to get them translated but didn't want to put them in the hands of someone else, in case they should be worth something. If I send them out, would you translate them for me?'

'Of course.' Sheelagh sat up, smiling. 'They sound interesting.'

'You type?'

'Yes, but not well.'

'That's okay, so long as I can read it. I'll send a typewriter, too.'

'And paper and ribbons,' she reminded him.

He chuckled. 'I won't forget. Right then, see you some time, Sheelagh. Come on, Luke.'

Sheelagh was looking at the tall, broad-shouldered man who stood there silently, staring out of the window at the blue ocean.

'See you, Sheelagh,' Luke said curtly, and followed the slow-moving, monstrously fat figure of Mercury as he wobbled down the stairs.

Sheelagh heard the roar of the car's engine. Then it went past and Mercury waved. Luke did not.

Then all was quiet – terribly, horribly quiet. She lay back in the chair, hands pressed to her eyes. This was her new life. Somehow she must learn to like it. Somehow.

'Madame? You wish to eat?' The voice brought Sheelagh out of her worried thoughts. She dropped her hands and looked up. A tall, stout woman stood before her. A big smile showed her flashing white teeth, while her coffee-coloured skin and bright curious eyes made her face something that was not easy to forget. She smiled sympathetically. 'Madame is tired. She wish to sleep? But Master Merk said she must have food. Here it is.'

'Master Merk?' Sheelagh sat up, shaking her head, brushing back her dust-laden hair.

'The big Master,' the woman explained, holding her hands out in front of her in a half circle.

Sheelagh caught herself laughing but managed to stop.

'You are?'

'Tarantula.'

Frowning, Sheelagh looked puzzled. 'But I thought Tarantula was a huge spider.'

Tarantula nodded her head so vigorously that Sheelagh thought the white scarf wrapped round and round the dark head would fall off. Instead the torn white apron did, sliding down the big body. Tarantula laughed.

'It always does,' she said, her voice resigned as she bent to pick up the white apron and tied it round her over her pink dress. 'That is so. Tarantula is a huge spider. Master Merk, he say I am a spider always leaving webs behind. My real name, it is Héloïse, but Monsieur, he does not like that either, so,' she shrugged as if sharing with Sheelagh the fact that men were strange creatures, 'I am Tarantula. You will eat?'

She pulled forward a trolley. On it was some delicious-looking seafood as well as salad. There was a small bell.

'You ring and I come,' said Tarantula, turning away, walking with big feet along the verandah, nearly tripping over a chair on her way, then vanishing out of sight.

Almost immediately as Sheelagh began to eat, suddenly realising that she was hungry, she could hear furniture being moved noisily around inside the house. Tarantula must be hastily cleaning! When Sheelagh had finished, she rang the little brass bell and Tarantula came pounding back, this time carrying a tray with a long glass, full of orange juice and ice.

'Madame is happy?' she asked. Her voice sounded anxious. 'Soon we will be very clean.' She pushed the trolley away.

'I'm fine,' Sheelagh smiled reassuringly. The ice cold drink was pleasant and she soon finished it. She could hear bangs coming from inside the house, then a low, singularly sweet voice singing. Tarantula was working hard, Sheelagh thought. Maybe it would be best to stay out where she was for a while and give Tarantula a chance to get on with it.

Sheelagh leant back in her chair, closing her eyes. When would Luke be back? And when he came...

When Sheelagh awoke, she sat very still for a few moments, trying to work out where she was. As she lay back in the chair, she could see through the screen that on the other side of the road in front of the house, there was a wide border of grass and of coconut trees. Everywhere there were coconut trees, she thought. On the other side of the wide border was the white sand, going in a long slope that ended abruptly by the line of rugged rocks. Some were queer shapes; some small, others pointed skywards as if angry, and against these rocks the sea came thundering in with long rollers, white-flecked with surf, for there was no lagoon here and the huge waves that came racing in had come for miles as if seeking something.

Slowly she stood up. Everything was quiet. Glancing at her watch, she was surprised at the time. She must have slept quite a while. It was very hot, though a fan in the ceiling was whirling round and round. Where was Tarantula? she wondered; probably asleep after her unexpected spurt of hard work.

Sheelagh walked down the wide screened verandah past the closed door that led into the house. The verandah ran right along the house and then down on the left, making it look like an L. There were long windows leading to the rooms within, and at least three French doors. Going close to the windows, she looked in, but the rooms looked dark so it was hard to see. Back she went to the front door, opening it, feeling strangely uncertain of herself. This had been another woman's home, she told herself, and now it was hers.

Inside the house there was a straight corridor, cutting it in half. On either side were three doors, facing one another across the passage. She hesitated as she wondered which side first, then decided on the right, as that had obviously been the sitting-room.

She opened the door and stood still, a little puzzled. She had expected dark antique furniture; instead it was Swedish type, modern, with a deep settee and four huge armchairs. Half the room was obviously used as a lounge. The curtains were dark blue, the walls an ugly red. She hated that on sight, but the furniture she liked. The other half of the room was the dining-room

– an oval table with four chairs and a large sideboard. Here again the colours were dark and depressing to look at. If the walls could be repainted and she made new curtains...

But would Luke mind? Would he see that as criticism of his choice, for it might have been the colours he liked and not the ones Georgina had chosen.

Somehow as Sheelagh stood there, looking round, Georgina became a real woman. An enemy. Someone to fear, because obviously Luke had not forgotten her even though it must be nearly eleven years since they parted.

Back into the hall went Sheelagh, opening the door opposite. It was the bedroom.

As soon as she saw it she liked the large dressing table with a huge heart-shaped mirror and the large wardrobes which matched the satin wood, but the curtains were a drab green, the walls bright pink, the bed...

It was the most enormous bed she had ever seen and was probably called a kingsize bed. At least it was a double one, she thought, so surely that night...

If only Luke would give her a chance to say how sorry she was. Sorry that she had come out with the question at such a time and in such a way. If only she had waited until the honeymoon was over and she could have said casually:

'Were you ever in love before, Luke?' and he could have laughed and said it was for a day only that his wife pretended she loved him. Sheelagh sighed. She could have sounded surprised, said she hadn't realised he was married, she was sorry it hadn't been a success. Then he could have told her Georgina had died. And Sheelagh thought, as she shook her head slowly, looking round the room, she could have asked even more casually, 'You had no children?' and Luke would have told her the truth. And everything would have been different, so very different.

If only...

Suddenly her eyes smarted and she walked across the room to a door. Had Luke a dressing-room? she wondered anxiously. In any case, the lounge had a couch. If only he would give her time to tell him how sorry she was...

It wasn't a dressing-room but a bathroom, a deep bath with a shower. It was clean and inviting on such a hot day, but she decided to see the whole house before she had a cool shower and unpacked her clothes.

Back to the corridor she went and down to the third door, the one that faced the door to the dining-room part of the main room. This was a kitchen, quite big and modern with a double sink, an electric cooker. Everything was clean.

Tarantula came up the steps that led to the ground at the back. Without apparently realising it, she spoke in French, quickly, eagerly, asking Sheelagh if her sleep had done her good and that she hoped she would be happy here and would live for many years.

It wasn't quite the French Sheelagh had been taught; it was a mixture of French, English and other languages, but she could understand and when she replied in French she saw the delight on Tarantula's face.

'It is good, this,' Tarantula told her. 'We shall be happy.'

Sheelagh hesitated. She was a wife now. Luke would be home for dinner, so shouldn't she do something about the evening meal?

She tried to explain her problem, but Tarantula's smile was huge as she said there was no need to worry. Always in the deep freeze was food, that she knew what Monsieur liked, and she would prepare it for them.

Sheelagh thanked her and went back to the bedroom, hastily undressing and going under the cool bliss of the shower. She washed her hair, too, combing it out afterwards, knowing that it would soon dry in the heat. Finding her dressing gown, she unpacked her clothes, grateful for the many hangers in the wardrobe.

Tarantula stood in the doorway, her eyes bright with interest as she said that this dress was beautiful and where had Madame bought it? Each dress she talked about, her voice eager as she asked questions.

'What will Madame wear?' she asked worriedly. 'It is so hot, but tonight it will be cooler. Madame would like some tea? *N'est-ce pas?*'

'I'd prefer coffee,' Sheelagh confessed, and Tarantula beamed.

'It is so with the monsieur. That is good this way,' she smiled, and hurried off.

At least Tarantula was her friend, Sheelagh thought as she decided to wear a thin silk kaftan. It was pink with huge sprawly but beautiful dark flowers embroidered on it.

She looked in the long mirror at herself. Her wet hair hung down her back as Luke liked it. She had used practically no make-up, a quick wisp of powder, her eyebrows but not her eyes, for Luke hated that.

She stopped dead, her hand with the eyebrow brush in it paused in mid-air, as she gazed at her face in the mirror. It was pathetic, she thought. Why, she looked scared to death, as if afraid to hope. Was she to spend the rest of her life fearful of Luke? Worrying what to say to him, afraid of how he would react? Was that marriage? Real marriage?

Barefooted, with the cool kaftan swinging gently, she went back to the verandah, walking round to stand in front of the main room, gazing thoughtfully at the shambles of what had once obviously been a beautiful garden. Now neglected, it looked a mess.

What would her father say? He would be horrified and almost at once, he would be out here himself, trying to sort something out of chaos. Could she do that? she wondered. If she was to be alone a lot, as both Luke and Mercury had said, she must have plenty of interests. But there again, this kind of life was so different from that in England. Would it be the gardener's job, not that of the lady of the house? Would Luke mind?

Sheelagh turned away angrily. It was becoming quite an obsession with her. After all, it was going to be as much her garden as Luke's, so surely she would have some say in what was done to it?

She went and sat down, gazing at the endless blue ocean and the waves that came racing in. She wondered what time it would be in England. Was it an hour behind or more? What would they be doing at home?

'Coffee, Madame.' Tarantula beamed as she spoke. There were a few shortbread biscuits on the plate. 'Tomorrow I will bake a cake,' Tarantula promised, and was gone before Sheelagh could speak.

As she slowly drank her coffee, Sheelagh's thoughts went home again. Would Dad be playing golf and her mother at one of her meetings? Or would he be in the garden, all alone?

As she was. She found herself twisting her engagement ring round. It was one large emerald, standing alone in its beauty. Now she stared at it ... could it have been Georgina's ring? Luke had not taken her with him to choose it. He had just produced it and she had loved it at once.

Now, sitting in a chair, probably chosen by Georgina, she could imagine the row they might have had, with Georgina saying *this* wasn't the life she had expected, nor was she going to live in such a jungle, angrily flinging her engagement ring on the floor. Was that what had happened? Was it this ring?

Was it? Sheelagh drank some more coffee. Then she remembered Luke had said that all Georgina wanted was money, so then it wasn't likely that Georgina would have thrown back an expensive ring!

Sighing with relief, Sheelagh scolded herself. It was becoming absolutely absurd. If only there was something she could do ... something to stop her from thinking such utterly stupid things. Luke wasn't the type of man to give his second wife the engagement ring he had given his first.

Or was he? That was what was frightening her and why they must talk it over, really get down to the roots of the whole thing. Luke had become a stranger. Before they were married she had never thought of that, but then marriage was different.

So what about the letter to her father? Luke still had it. Would he have read it? If so what had he thought of it? Sheelagh worried. Had he really believed she was going to run him down to her father? Telling him the whole story?

She must write again, because if her father got no card or letter he would worry, ring up one of the hotels she was supposed to be staying at and when he found they weren't there, he might panic and start a search or something awful.

There was a walnut desk in the dining-room part of the main room. In it she found paper and overseas airmail envelopes. She sat down and wrote.

Somehow this letter was easier than the one before. She simply explained they had decided to postpone their honeymoon.

'This is the most beautiful and amazing island. A real mix-up – lovely trees, super flowers – the funny little yellow one would fascinate you. It's got a funny name that I can't remember, but they grow out of stunted trees, Dad. Luke says you must come out and see us as they grow masses of the most gorgeous orchids and he'd like your advice. I have a very amusing maid called Tarantula. Mercury, he's Luke's partner, called her that because she leaves *webs* behind! I didn't understand at first, but she's always dropping things or leaving the chair crooked or falling over, so you know she's been around. I have the most superb view of the Indian Ocean, huge waves pounding the rocks. The garden has been rather neglected, but I think it will be fun to put it right...' she began writing. Suddenly there was so much she could tell her father, knowing the beautifully relaxed feeling that nothing she said could be wrong or would annoy him.

It was getting dark when all the lights came on. The little house must look like a jewel, she thought, in the darkness. She finished the letter and went back to her seat on the front verandah, waiting for the sound of his car, yet in a way dreading it, hoping that this time she wouldn't say the wrong thing.

Tarantula came with a tray on which were cold drinks and bottles of brandy and whisky as well as a silver bowl full of ice cubes.

Was that one of Luke's first wedding presents? Sheelagh wondered, and then deliberately changed her thoughts, for it was becoming an absolute obsession with her. She must make herself stop thinking about Georgina.

It wasn't much fun drinking alone, she thought, but after a while she poured herself a gin and lime, leaning back. How quiet it was, she was thinking when suddenly the shrill whirring of the cicadas began. At least that was something! Would the radio work here? she wondered. She must ask Luke.

She had so much to ask him. Was that why he was staying away? Because he didn't want to answer the questions? Yet he must.

Was she always going to be alone for hours on end like this? If so, she must plan something to do – some really engrossing hobby that could fill the gap. For she was not used to loneliness, at all. But she would adjust... If Mercury remembered to send those manuscripts, they might prove fascinating, then if she gardened, too, and next time she was near the shops, if ever she was, she would buy paints, for there was so much in this beauty she would like to paint.

She was in the bedroom, brushing her hair, when she heard the car come. She stood very still, listening to the slamming of the car door, the bang of the screened door, his footsteps on the steps outside, then the hall door. She waited, staring at the door.

But Luke didn't appear. He walked down the passage, shouting for Tarantula, then after speaking to her he went outside to the verandah.

Sheelagh stood very still. Why didn't he come to look for her? Didn't he want to see her?

What should she do? Show her disinterest in him as well? Go to bed quickly and pretend to be asleep?

But that might ruin it for ever. She put down the hairbrush, patted her hair, as it wasn't quite dry, and went outside to the verandah.

Luke was sprawling in an armchair, paper in one hand, glass in the other. He looked up.

'Hallo,' he said casually, standing up. 'Can I get you a drink? Sorry I'm so late – a real mess-up over at the hotel. You like gin and lime, don't you?'

'Yes, please,' Sheelagh said as she sat down. As if he didn't know! Why was he talking like this, just as if they had met by accident? 'Had a bad day?' she asked, with equal indifference.

He grinned and she knew they must find a way to stop this nonsense. She loved him too much to bear it.

'Not really. It often happens. Difficult hotel guest, swears there's thieves about as she lost her ring, creates hell and then finds she's got the ring in her handbag. Never an apology.' He laughed, drained his glass and refilled it. 'What have you been doing? Must have been pretty boring.'

'I met Tarantula and looked around,' Sheelagh told him, gulping down her drink and wishing something would tell her when the right moment came. Somehow it didn't seem that this was, for she could hear Tarantula

121

thumping round in the long main room, probably laying the table for dinner. Later, when they were on their own, she decided.

'Like the furniture?' he asked.

'Very much,' she said, glad she could say this truthfully. She just stopped herself in time from asking if it had been Georgina's choice. How lucky it was she realised in a few minutes, for Luke went on:

'As soon as we got engaged, the next time I was out here I got rid of the old stuff and bought this. Actually,' he looked at her and for a moment, she thought it was a rueful smile, 'I had arranged for the rooms to be repainted while we were on our honeymoon. Now, at least, you can say what colours you'd like. I must say, it was a mess – or rather, it is. Sorry about that.'

She was so happy she wanted to sing. None of the furniture was Georgina's. It had been bought for her!

'We'll soon get it looking different,' she said eagerly, and then hesitated. Was that a criticism of what it was? Yet he had said that. 'I … I must admit I don't like the colours.'

Luke chuckled. 'Actually there's quite a story about that,' he began, just as Tarantula came flouncing out, a clean untorn apron already sliding down her huge hips. 'Dinner.

Come along,' he said, leading the way.

Tarantula was a good cook. It was a very nice curry, the rice perfectly cooked. There was a silence as Tarantula served vegetables.

'You were saying there was a funny story,' Sheelagh began, hating the silence in case it should continue indefinitely.

Luke laughed. 'Yes. It happened about two years ago. I wasn't well. It was before we met. They thought it was malaria, but it wasn't. Anyhow, I had to go to the mainland to hospital and some of the men who work for me here decided to make me a present of a *newly-painted house*. I agree it needed a new painting, but...' He chuckled. 'It *is* pretty miserable, but I could hardly repaint it, could I?'

'I can see that. But won't it offend or hurt them if we do now?' Sheelagh asked.

He shook his head. 'No, this is different. A man should paint his house for his bride. What colours had you in mind?'

They discussed colours while they ate, then had a strawberry jelly.

'Tarantula has done well,' Sheelagh commented.

'Oh, we always keep a deep freeze and pantry well stocked. I can never tell when Mercury will turn up with guests.'

'But you've been away so long.'

'That doesn't worry him. He'd rather entertain here when I'm away than use his own house.'

'But why?'

'It's a long story,' he said, getting up. 'Some other time.' He looked at his watch. 'I must be off.'

'You're going – again?' Sheelagh couldn't keep the dismay out of her voice.

Luke smiled at her. 'I'm sorry,' he said, and it sounded as if he meant it. 'It's a horrible way of spending your first day here. Unfortunately this will always happen, Sheelagh, so maybe it's best for you to know how things will be from the word go. I won't be late, I promise you.'

He stood by her side and gently stroked her hair. It seemed hours since he had touched her. It was all she could do not to jump up and fling her arms round his neck, bursting into tears. Yet this was the wrong moment, for he had already left her, letting the door slam behind him.

She sat very still, her eyes closed tight, because she didn't want Tarantula to see her in tears.

Sheelagh was sitting upright in the chair on the verandah when Luke came home. She was wearing her pretty pink nightie and jacket and had not dared to go to bed in case she fell asleep. All the same, it had been a battle to stay awake in the chair, but she knew something had to be done that night if her marriage was to be a happy one.

Luke came hurrying up the steps. 'Why on earth did you wait up for me?' he asked, sounding annoyed. 'Go along to bed while I just finish reading this.' He waved a paper in his hand.

Slowly Sheelagh stood up. She felt absurdly wobbly on her legs, her eyes were half closed. But something had to be done *then*. It was always *later*.

'Luke, I've got to talk to you,' she said. 'Now.'

He frowned. 'I won't be ten minutes with this, but...'

She moved forward suddenly, snatching the piece of paper out of his hand, flinging it to the ground. 'I insist on talking to you now! I'm fed up to the teeth with this later you always say. I tried to talk to you yesterday, but you wouldn't let me tell you what I've got to tell you...' She stopped, her voice sounding desperate to her.

It seemed it did to him, too. 'What have you got to tell me?' he asked, and moved forward, his hands clutching her shoulders, his fingers digging into her flesh.

His face had changed colour; he looked white, as if he was shocked.

'All right, tell me,' he said bitterly. 'You're just like Georgina. You've discovered you don't love me and you hate this place!'

Sheelagh was so startled she could hardly speak. 'No, I don't. I *love* the place. It's beautiful.' Her words seemed to tumble over themselves as if she was afraid to stop speaking. 'Luke, I've *got* to tell you. I'm sorry, I'm most terribly sorry. I realise I shouldn't have asked you that question and ... and ... I can't bear it, Luke. I love you so much and you just won't ... you just won't...' Her eyes were smarting with unshed tears and suddenly her voice dwindled away.

He bent down towards her. 'You do love me?' he said slowly.

'I love you so much, and I don't mind if you've had a hundred wives. Yes, I do.' Her voice changed. 'Because I'm jealous.' Again her voice broke. 'That's what it is – I'm just jealous. I hate the thought of you loving anyone else. That's what it is, Luke..'

Suddenly he lifted her in his arms, his mouth brushing her cheeks. 'My little Sheelagh,' he said, his voice wondering. 'You really mean it, don't you? You are jealous?'

Her arms went round his neck. 'I know I'm ... I'm being unfair. That it all happened years ago, but ... but, Luke, I think you're still in love with her, and that's what frightens me.'

'In love with who?' he asked, carrying her down the verandah towards the door.

'Georgina, of course.'

'Oh, her!' he said scornfully. 'I forgot her years ago. It's us, now, Sheelagh. Just *us.*'

He kicked open the bedroom door and carried her into the room, dropping her on to the huge bed, then sat by her side, leaning over her, tracing the features of her face with his finger gently. 'You said you wanted to talk? You've questions you want me to answer?'

His mouth was so close to hers, she could feel the warmth of his breath.

'It can wait, Luke, darling,' she said, pulling him closer, her mouth kissing the corners of his lips. 'We'll talk tomorrow. Let's just be us.'

He laughed and pulled her up in his arms.

'I couldn't agree more,' he said joyfully.

'What about the paper you wanted to read?' she asked, her eyes dancing.

'That! It can wait. This is more important,' he said. He looked down at her, her face so near his. 'Did you really think I still loved Georgina?'

She nodded. 'I don't think I've been really *thinking*. I was just scared you still loved her and not me.'

'You'll know,' Luke said as his arms tightened round her. 'You'll know all right,' he promised.

CHAPTER 5

Sheelagh awoke to the sound of Tarantula's clumsiness as she nearly fell over the chair near the door when leaving the room. Half asleep, she felt Luke's arms go round her and his mouth on her cheek.

'Wakey, wakey!' he teased.

'What's the time?' She turned and their mouths met.

It was quite a while before she could speak again.

'Really, Sheelagh, our coffee will be cold,' said Luke, pretending it was *her* fault he had spent so long kissing her.

'It's only six o'clock,' Sheelagh said, startled.

'I know. I left a note in the kitchen, asking Tarantula to call us at this time. You see, we won't be disturbed, and all those questions that were troubling you can be answered.' His arms pulled her close again and coffee was forgotten once more.

At last they drank it, propped up by pillows, Luke looking even more massive with his broad chest on which the fair hairs hardly showed.

'Well,' he said with a smile, 'let's start.' He put down his cup. 'Just one more kiss.'

She went into his arms happily. The night that had gone had shown her how gentle he could be, yet how passionate, how understanding, yet a man in every respect. Never had she thought it possible to love anyone so much.

'I could kiss you for hours,' he murmured, stroking her hair.

'I don't mind,' she said, laughing.

He pushed her away gently. 'No, Sheelagh. Let's get those questions that troubled you answered. You're going to be alone an awful lot and this gives you time to worry about something that isn't happening. Now, question one.' His hand moved down her arms as he drew her close to his side. 'Go ahead. Ask me anything you like.' He turned and kissed her. 'Sorry, I thought we weren't going to kiss any more.'

She began to laugh. '*You* kissed me!'

'Then it's your turn to kiss me,' he said triumphantly. 'By the way, before I forget it, I posted your letter to your father, and...' his mouth traced the line of her cheekbones, 'I didn't read it.'

'You could have, Luke. I said we'd decided to come here owing to circumstances beyond our control – that was always Dad's and my joke – and I said how beautiful the islands were.'

'Well, I asked him to arrange for our wedding presents to be crated and sent out here. I also asked them both out to visit us.'

'But we've only one bedroom,' Sheelagh said quickly, not sure suddenly if she wanted her parents to come out so soon.

'Mercury will lend us his house. That way we'll still be on our own.'

She turned to kiss him. 'You always read my thoughts.'

'Don't tempt me, Mrs Jessop,' he teased, gently pushing her away. 'I'm very susceptible to kisses. Now the questions. First?'

'Viola. Why is she so...'

'Bitchy? I don't know. Maybe she was born that way. I've known her for thirteen years. I

130

told you how I was tossed from one reluctant aunt to another and then broke away? I met Mercury and he offered me a job in Madagascar. I was a young, lonely bachelor with little money and their frequent invitations to dinner were a great help.'

'Viola fancied you?' Sheelagh teased.

'She may have done. She was six years older than me, but I was a useful escort. I certainly had no feelings that way for her. Gina was at the same school as Viola, a young new girl when Viola was a prefect, and they kept in touch always – so when Gina had an unhappy love affair, the Whittakers asked her out to stay. Then I met her.'

'And fell in love?' Sheelagh tried to keep the jealousy out of her voice.

He turned and kissed her. 'I doubt it. Admittedly I liked her, her gay laughter. The moments when she cried, I wanted to make her happy.' He gave a little grunt. 'What a fool I was! I don't think Viola ever forgave us. I'll never forget her face when we announced our engagement. Mercury told me I was mad, but he gave me a far more responsible job on this island with bigger salary. He loaned me money so I could buy furniture for this house. I got it all ready – my first home. I was proud of it.' His fingers gently patted Sheelagh's arm and she closed her eyes.

'How Gina ever got the idea that I was Mercury's heir, I don't know. Maybe Viola invented it to ruin our marriage.' He gave another little grunt. 'She succeeded all right. Gina was horrified when she saw the island. Mind you, the roads were much worse in those days, because we'd only just taken over the island and there was much to be done. When she saw Mercury's house, she literally jumped for joy. Now that was the house of her dreams, she said. It hurt like hell to have to admit it wasn't our home. When she saw this ... you can imagine how she felt. Everything she hated – the furniture I had bought but could ill afford, the garden I'd hastily made, everything.'

He paused and sighed. 'Maybe she was right and I was wrong. Maybe it was asking too much of a girl to live my way of life.'

'If she loved you...'

Luke turned his head and smiled. 'She didn't, you see. She told me that. We had a terrific row, she accused me of lying, of letting her believe I was Mercury's heir. She told me she'd only married me for my money, that she still loved her other boy-friend. Well, transport was much worse then and the next boat went out in a week, so she had to stay with me. In the end, we had a sort of truce and decided to try and make a go of it. I think Mercury, who visited us, must have reassured her about my financial future. Anyhow, then Viola visited her while I was away, five months after our marriage. And one month later Gina left me. She never said why. I didn't even know she was pregnant.'

Sheelagh was stroking his hand, not looking at him, ashamed of the jealousy she felt. 'But you loved her?'

'I don't know. It was nice coming back to someone and not an empty house. Better a row than silence, I thought then. It was absolute hell when she went. Let's forget, Sheelagh. I've forgotten her long ago.' He turned and took Sheelagh in his arms. 'I love you. Remember that – always.'

'I promise,' she whispered as she kissed him. But still that little acid fear stayed inside her. Luke *had* loved Gina, still remembered her. This was something Sheelagh knew she would have to learn to live with.

'I was a fool to marry so young or someone so young,' Luke said. 'Today I wouldn't do it.'

'But you married me, and I'm only twenty,'

Sheelagh teased.

'You're different,' he said, and for a moment she believed he meant it.

'If this was your home, how was it you were in England so long?' Sheelagh asked casually.

'Well, you know I told you I'd had that mysterious fever that they thought was malaria but wasn't? I was sent to a specialist who suggested I got out of the country for a spell, so Mercury put me on a job for him in England. I came out to test and now they think I'm okay.'

'You love it here?' Sheelagh held his hand against her cheek.

He smiled. 'I do, but I doubt if I would if I had to be here all the time. Since Mercury's got so enormous he dislikes travelling, so I do a lot for him, and at any time I may have to go to New York, Timbuktu or anywhere. Now it'll be even more fun, because you'll come with me. Okay?'

'I'll love it,' she said eagerly.

His arm tightened round her. 'You still feel I've deserted my daughter?'

Sheelagh looked at him quickly, suddenly fearful and then relieved as she saw the same tender lovable Luke, and not the difficult man he had been the day before.

'I don't think you've deserted her. I'm just sorry for her as ... well, you know how I feel about Dad.'

'I do.' For a moment there was a hard note in Luke's voice, but it vanished. 'All girls don't feel that way. Look, love, here I was, on this even more deserted island in those days. What could I do with an eighteen-month-old child? And when it came to education, she'd have to go to boarding school. The Hamiltons, Gina's parents, are a very nice couple. I've met them. I've seen Zoe quite often. I go to speech days and sports days at her school, I even went once to see her act in a school play. I send her presents from Uncle L. This was Mrs Hamilton's idea. She says that when Zoe's education is over, she should be told and then come and visit me. We haven't met, nor has Zoe ever seen me, I think. She's very like her mother, with the same big nose. I only hope it doesn't worry her as much as it did Gina.'

Again Sheelagh knew a surge of shameful jealousy, for the way his voice changed when he said *Gina* told her so much. He might not realise it, but Luke had loved Gina and still remembered her.

'Love.' Sheelagh turned to kiss the corners of his mouth, feeling his arms going round her. 'Just one more question, but I'm afraid to ask it in case you throw me out as you did before.'

He laughed. 'I'm in a good mood today, love. Go ahead.'

'Why ... why were you so angry when I asked about Zoe?' Sheelagh asked a little nervously.

'Maybe because I've never been sure I'm doing the right thing for Zoe. Maybe also because I was in a bad mood already. Viola had made me so angry. She spoke to me at our reception, you see. That's why I wanted us to hurry away, because I was afraid she'd speak to you. I was too late. The damage was done.'

'What did she say to you?'

'She told me you were too young and immature and that life on this island would have the same effect on you as it had on Gina.'

'Was that why we came out here instead of...'

'Rome, etc? Partly. I had to prove she was wrong. Maybe I was a fool even to listen to her, but walking down the aisle towards me, you'd looked so terrified I wondered if you were too young and I was expecting too much of you. That maybe it wasn't fair.

Another thing was that the way you threw the question at me reminded me of Gina. It was just the same – as if the words had exploded and you had to say them. The nightmare threatened to start again, scene after scene. Looking back, I've often wondered if Gina enjoyed them. I didn't and still don't. It didn't help things when you were so quiet on the planes, and on the boat you spoke only to Mercury. I began to wonder if you were already regretting it.'

Sheelagh threw her arms round his neck. 'You absolute idiot! It was *you* who didn't talk. *You* read and read the papers, *you* left me alone with Mercury and he just wouldn't stop talking. All the time I wanted us to be alone, I wanted to throw my arms round your neck and tell you I loved you.'

'Why didn't you?'

'Because we were never alone, and when we were, you treated me just as if I wasn't there. I thought you were so angry with me that you would never love me again.'

'You're the idiot,' he said softly as he kissed her. 'Was I really such a ... a monster?'

'You were, you know. I was almost scared to open my mouth. It was ... I hate to say this, Luke, but it was ... well, ghastly.'

'I'm sorry. So very sorry. Let's face it, I've

got a foul temper. Usually I can control it. If I have a real problem – I had plenty yesterday apart from my anxiety about you - I'm apt to retreat into a secret world of my own and completely forget those outside it. I'm sorry, but that's the way I'm made.'

'Now I know I can understand.' She rubbed her cheek against his. 'Oh, Luke, I'm so happy, so very happy.'

'You won't be lonely or bored?' he asked anxiously.

She smiled. 'I'm determined not to be. Mercury's manuscripts may be interesting, then I'd love to get to work on the garden. I'd also like to start painting and ... oh, just one thing, Luke, I would love a dog. I've never had a dog of my own.'

'Any particular kind?'

'I don't mind. Just something little and lovable, then he'll keep me company.'

'You shall have a dozen dogs if you like,' he said, laughing.

There was a sudden clanging of a bell. Luke frowned.

'Breakfast! How time flies!' He turned and took Sheelagh in his arms, kissing her tenderly. 'Love, I'll try to be back for lunch. If I can't make it, forgive me. Anyhow, we'll have a long quiet evening alone. I've an appointment in forty minutes.' He leapt out of the bed, turning to kiss her again, a long lingering kiss, before standing up. 'I'll tell Tarantula to bring you your breakfast. Boiled eggs, exactly three minutes, right?' he said with a smile, and hurried into the bathroom.

Sheelagh lay very still. She was so happy she wanted to cry. They had talked – that was the important thing. Now she knew what she was up against. But her greatest enemy was herself! Her jealousy of Gina, who had been dead for years.

CHAPTER 6

Often Sheelagh had heard her father talk about the importance of *dialogue* and the *ability to communicate*, particularly in marriage, he had said once, but she had never understood what he meant until the morning after the night when her marriage had ceased to be 'in name only'. The long talk with Luke that early morning had made her realise just how stupidly melodramatic she had been about everything. His gentleness, his patience in explaining things had driven out the foolish fears she had known. Now that he had warned her about his *moods*, she felt she would be able to cope all right.

But as the days became weeks, she was to find it was not all as easy as it sounded. Her new life was so completely different from the life she had known that she had to make many adjustments.

Loneliness was the biggest obstacle to happiness, because Luke was out nearly all day, usually late for meals, or too moody to talk to. Gradually, though, things improved. She learned to keep silent when he was in one of his moods, she would pretend to read or do some of the knitting she was doing, and see that his glass was filled and just hope he would soon be over the 'problem'. Other evenings he came back, full of life, turning on the record player and insisting that they danced with the lights low. These happy evenings more than made up for the others, Sheelagh felt, as gradually she filled her days with jobs.

Mercury had sent her the manuscripts, a typewriter, paper, ribbons, and carbons. He had also sent her an easel and oil paints with a short note wishing her good luck. In addition they had two garden boys, not very old but willing to learn.

Most successful of all cures of loneliness was the dog, a small cuddly black little dachshund with long flapping ears, amazing courage and the habit of curling up by her foot, his head on her toe. Jackie, she called him, because like the Jack of *Jack and the Beanstalk*, little Jackie tackled everything, giving a little squeal if he fell over yet jumping up to race around, his little tail wagging fast.

Sheelagh had a letter from her father. At first he had sounded puzzled, worried because she had not had a proper honeymoon.

'The best time to get to know one another,' he had written.

Would it have been? Sheelagh often wondered. Would she have got to know the real Luke as she was doing now?

However, after receiving several happy letters from Sheelagh, her father seemed to have accepted it and was suggesting that he and her mother might come out the following year.

'I'd like to come sooner, Sheelagh, but I think a newly married couple should be left alone together for a while.'

When they were together, she would think sometimes as in the early hours of the morning, while it was still cool, she and Jackie walked round the garden, telling Pierre and Henri where to dig up the weeds, how to make a compost heap, and plant cuttings. This was all new to her, but Luke had brought home a *Farmer's Weekly* to study. In addition, she had a car, a small bright red car in which one day Luke sat by her side letting her drive. At first she had felt unsure, because the car was so different from her father's, but when Luke said quietly: 'Not to worry. We all stall in new cars and make mistakes. Just get used to it and at ease,' she had driven, and as time passed she found complete self-confidence. Then Luke showed her the shorter drive to the small town where they had landed. This meant that Sheelagh could drive in whenever she liked. Not that there was much to see when she did, for the shops had little to offer and it was more usual to send orders to Moroni.

'We're planning a big store,' Luke told her, 'but at the moment there aren't enough people living here to make it worth while.'

'But wouldn't the tourists buy things from it?' Sheelagh asked, curled up on the couch one evening.

'The hotel has its own shop,' Luke explained. 'Tourists usually want souvenirs.

The locals make a lot of them and can earn extra money that way.'

Sometimes Luke talked about his work, but he seemed to prefer to forget it when he came home in the evenings. This was inclined to worry Sheelagh, so one night, as they ate Tarantula's well-cooked meal, she looked at him.

'Luke, why don't you talk about your work? I am interested, you know.'

'Because I have it all day and want to forget it.' He leant across the table, putting his hand over hers. 'I like to come home and have you tell me about what you've done all day. Sure you're not bored?'

Sheelagh laughed. 'I haven't time to be bored, what with Jackie to exercise before it gets too hot, the garden, my painting, the manuscripts, the day flies by.'

'You don't miss me?' Luke pulled a long face and pretended to cry.

'Idiot!' Sheelagh said with a laugh. 'I miss you all the time.'

'I'm glad,' he told her, and then laughed. 'I am selfish, aren't I?'

Everything seemed to be going well, Sheelagh was thinking one day when she was painting a beautiful but leafless tree with expressive branches that reminded her of hungry arms, imploring for food, while on the ground around were masses of flowers that seemed far from hungry. Jackie was curled up on the ground by her side, his eyes closed, but when Sheelagh moved, Jackie's little tail would wag quickly. Tarantula came puffing out to the end verandah, carrying Sheelagh's ice-filled drink, tripping as usual over something that wasn't there and shooting the glass to the ground.

Jackie squealed and ran down the verandah, limping, his tail between his legs, so Sheelagh dropped everything and ran after him.

He had squeezed right underneath a tallboy in the corner. The bottom of it came low to the ground and Sheelagh had difficulty in coaxing Jackie out, for he had to lie down quite flat, legs outstretched. He came out backwards, wriggling hard, his little tail first, and then Sheelagh could gently help by pulling him. Finally he came out, head down, long ears flat, while in his mouth between his prickly little teeth, he clutched a small bundle, dropping it by Sheelagh, looking up at her, leaping to lick her cheek, seemingly proud of himself.

Sheelagh picked up the bundle and was about to throw it in the waste paper basket when something slid out. She bent to pick it up and saw it was a photograph – the photograph of a girl.

Tarantula had returned with another cold drink, full of apologies and fussing over Jackie. Almost automatically Sheelagh took the glass in her hands, the bundle and photograph in the other, and walked to a chair and sat down.

She knew whose photograph it was. It could only be Gina's. As she stared at it, she understood how Luke, a lonely bachelor, could have fallen in love. Gina might not be beautiful and perhaps her nose was a little big, but her eyes were bright and she had a lovely smile. Sheelagh could imagine her laughing and teasing. That was how Gina was before ... before? Was it before Viola was jealous and tried to ruin the marriage and succeeded? Sheelagh shivered. Because thanks to her own foolishness, her marriage had been nearly ruined too. Thanks be that Viola was thousands of miles away and could not hurt them now.

She looked at the package, pushed the photograph back into it and saw that the rest of the contents were letters. It was a strangely thin spidery writing, taking up a lot of space. She was tempted to read them, very tempted indeed.

But how would she feel if Luke came across some of Tony's passionate love letters and read them? Not that she had kept them. That part of her life was over and she had no desire to be reminded ... Sheelagh was thinking, and her mind seemed to come to an abrupt halt. Slowly she went over her thoughts:

That part of her life was over and she had no desire to be reminded.

Luke had said the same. That was the past, he had said, we must forget it.

Yet he had kept Gina's photograph and letters!

Somehow she got up and walked to the tallboy, Jackie close behind her, his little tail wagging. She bent and pulled open the bottom drawer. It was stiff and she had to tug hard, but at last she got it open. A mixture of things was inside it – a hairbrush, jars of face creams, papers, make-up, just as if someone had swept everything off a dressing-table and thrown it in. At the back of the drawer, part of the floor had fallen away. The letters must have fallen through that ... but if so, then whose letters were they, and why were they with Gina's photograph?

Sheelagh closed the drawer and stood up.

She looked at the painting she had done. It was terrible, she thought. The tree no more looked like a starving creature than it did a tree. Furious with it and with herself, she seized a palette knife, swept all the paints on her palette together and splashed it all over the canvas until she had used up every bit of paint she had put out. She was angry – angry with herself. How could she be so jealous of someone who had died eight or nine years ago? How could she? Yet she was.

Her father had always told her that jealousy was the most dangerous and vile disease in the world. Was she suffering from it, Sheelagh wondered, or did you always feel like this when you loved someone?

'Come on, Jackie,' she said. 'Let's get out of here.'

They went to the kitchen. 'I'll be out to lunch, Tarantula,' Sheelagh said in French. 'Tell the Master when he comes in ... if he does,' she added. There was that chance and she didn't want to risk it.

Whatever happened she mustn't see Luke while she felt like this. If she did, she would probably make the terrible mistake she had on her wedding night, flinging the question at him the way Gina would have done, as Luke had thought.

Yet if he had forgotten her, why were Gina's things still in the tallboy? The tallboy must have been in the house at the time, yet Luke had said he had sold everything and bought new furniture for her, Sheelagh thought.

Perhaps driving into town with Jackie and having lunch at the new restaurant that had just been built might help her overcome this dreadful jealousy inside her.

But it didn't. As she drove carefully over the winding mountainous roads, Jackie asleep by her side, Sheelagh's mind seemed unable to forget the tallboy, the things that were Gina's in the bottom drawer, and she wondered whose letters they were. Certainly not from Luke, for his writing was very different, almost square with strength in each letter.

She reached the small town and was driving slowly along as the locals had a habit of wandering across the road as if unaware that there were such things as cars, and looking round, startled, when you sounded the horn. She was just passing the market, trying to remember where Luke had said the new restaurant was, when she caught her breath with dismay, for standing by a stall covered with paw-paws, bananas and other fruit, she saw Mercury! It would be difficult not to see him, for he stood in the blazing sun in his white suit, no hat on his bald head. And by Mercury's side was Luke!

Knowing she was in no mood to cope with either, Sheelagh hastily braked and managed to turn down a narrow side street and go out of the town again.

Jackie yawned, looking up at her with his little black twinkling eyes. 'Sorry, love,' said Sheelagh. 'We'll find somewhere to eat.' But where? There were few restaurants on the island and, as far as she knew, none outside the small towns. Should she go to the hotel? – but that was out, for surely if Mercury had arrived that day – which he must have done or Luke would have mentioned him – they would go straight to the hotel.

She drove along the coast, seeing parts of the island she had never seen before, some so lovely, some so barren, so eerie in the deadness from the hot volcanic lava that had fallen years before. Having given up hope finally of every finding anywhere to eat, Sheelagh discovered a small cove with a little square house, looking out at the ocean, which was still as here the lagoon was small and encircled by the coral reef. There was a little notice on a piece of wood, outside the house, saying 'BED AND BOARD'.

It was so very English in an island that was much more French that Sheelagh was drawn towards it. She parked the car and with Jackie running round in circles, his little tail wagging happily, Sheelagh went to the house.

A very old woman with sun-tanned skin, snow-white hair and a smile came to greet her in the hall.

'Could I have some lunch? Or just sandwiches and fruit?'

'Just a minute, dear,' the old woman said, fumbling in the pocket of her dark green cotton dress for her glasses, putting them on and peering at Sheelagh. 'Of course you can have lunch, dear. I've some cold ham and salad, and your little doggie ... what a darling! Do come in. Are you a tourist? We don't get many, I'm afraid.'

She led the way into the front room. It was cool with a fan whirring noisily, very clean and neat with just three small tables.

'What did you say your name was, dear?' the old woman asked after she had told Sheelagh to sit down, hurried out to the kitchen, calling to someone, and coming back to sit down opposite her. 'Mind if I join you? I see so few new faces it's a real joy. You're...?'

'Sheelagh Jessop.'

The old woman leaned forward, peering closer. 'But you can't be Luke's daughter. You're too old for that.'

'I'm his wife,' Sheelagh explained, feeling rather like a butterfly pinned to an observation board.

'You are? I heard he was married. But you're so young!'

'I'm twenty!' Sheelagh was rather indignant.

The old woman chuckled. 'You girls all look so young these days. I'm Martha Nucket. I've known Luke ever since he first came here. Sad, that about his wife. Of course, they should never have been married, both of them little more than children.'

A tall thin girl in a dark blue dress and spotlessly white apron brought in two plates of food, and a smaller one of chopped meat for Jackie, who rushed at it, sniffed it, looked up at Sheelagh for reassurance, and then dived into it, holding the plate firm with one paw.

The ham was fresh, the salad had little lettuce but plenty of tomatoes.

'You knew Luke's first wife?' Sheelagh asked, trying to sound casual although she had fought with herself, for she felt it wasn't a good idea to ask such a question. Suppose Luke found out? He would think she was snooping. Which, of course, she was, though it had begun unintentionally.

'Oh, yes, my dear. My husband and I have lived here for fifty years.'

'Fifty years?' Sheelagh's voice was shocked. How could anyone live on this tiny island for so long?

'Yes, and no regrets. He was keen on treasure hunting and we were just wed – I come from Somerset and he from Cheshire. He said one day we might be millionaires, so we took a chance and came.' She laughed, a happy laugh. 'And look at us, living in a rent-free cottage because of Luke's kindness, my old man not so active but still fishing and me running this, more to see people than earn any money.'

'You get many visitors?'

'I'm afraid not. You see, most go straight to the hotel. I told Luke only t'other day he should build some holiday flats, for it isn't all people what want to go to hotels, or can afford it. It certainly is nice to meet you, my dear. I hope you and Luke will be very happy. Poor Luke!' She shook her head. 'That was a bad mistake he made, marrying that girl. Not that we blamed him. He was young and lonely and she was a lovely girl.'

'She was?' Sheelagh felt the jealousy growing inside her again. 'Luke said she had a big nose.'

Mrs Nucket chuckled. 'That was what she was always saying, but we guessed it was just to make people look at her and say it wasn't big. A real egoist, that girl. All she could think of was money – about the only thing Luke hadn't got. He was such a thin lad. Tall, like a lathe. We all liked him, the few of us living here. Besides, Mercury's ideas for the island meant more work for the locals, and the poor dears needed it, fishing was the only thing here before Mercury took over. What do you think of him?' Mrs Nucket chuckled again. 'A real eyesore, eh? Yet when you know him...'

'You're so right,' Sheelagh said eagerly. 'At first I thought he was against me.'

'Against you?' Mrs Nucket rang a bell and the maid took the empty plates away and brought back jelly.

Sheelagh hesitated. It sounded so absurd when it was put into words, yet at the time it had seemed so real. 'I felt ... I had an idea he disapproved of me.'

'That's a joke of his. He likes to see how people react. He's got no time for a yes-man or a soft woman. Got the sweetest wife, but she can't understand him. His acts frighten her and he doesn't mean 'em.' She peered at Sheelagh. 'Men are strange cattle, my dear. You have to make allowances for their strange behaviour.'

Laughing, Sheelagh agreed. 'I'm learning that.'

'Nice lad, Luke. You're a lucky girl, but he can fly off the handle, just as if he's bottled up his anger and frustration and the final last straw sets off an explosion. We were all sorry for him, when his wife – I should say first wife – left him. He was so lonely. Not right for a young man like that to live alone, and he so good to her. She had real tantrums, just like a baby, screaming and throwing things about so they couldn't get anyone to work for them. That made things worse. Then this friend of hers came to stay.' Mrs Nucket shook her head sadly. 'That was the beginning of the end. We all knew except Luke, it seemed. He should have been more wary, for he knew the friend and what she was like, but he's one of those folk who have ideals, if you know what I mean. He trusts people – or leastways he did in those days. You finding it very lonely? Nice having a little car.'

Sheelagh told her how the day passed and

the old woman nodded approvingly. 'You're a sensible girl, dear. You'll always be welcome here, you know, when you feel like a chat. My Ernie is out all day and it's good to talk to someone young.'

'Thank you,' Sheelagh smiled. 'I often long for someone to talk to, too. How do I get back? I don't have to go right round?'

'Certainly not, my dear. When you go, I'll draw a little map for you, but don't hurry. There's coffee to come.'

'Lovely! Look, Mrs Nucket, didn't Luke realise Viola was causing trouble?'

'So you've met her, too? My dear, run a mile when you see her coming. That woman's real evil. She used to drive round the island with Gina and say how ghastly it was. Nothing here was right. I remember they came to me once for coffee. She – not Gina, but she sent back the coffee three times because it wasn't to her liking. She was that sort, and she was determined to wreck Luke's marriage.'

'I'd have thought he'd have noticed it. I mean, he's no fool.'

'You're so right! Point was, he was away for most of that month. Mercury had sent him off to America on a course of some kind, and that horrible woman seized her chance and came to stay with Gina. Soon after she'd gone and Luke was back, Gina walked out.'

'He loved her?' Sheelagh asked, then wished she hadn't.

'Yes and no,' Mrs Nucket said. 'She was a lovely girl, laughing a lot, but always showing off. They used to quarrel all the time – leastways she did. 'Twas a good thing for Luke when she went, for he has a quick temper and we could see he was fighting to control it. What she needed was to be put over his knee and given a good spanking!'

Sheelagh found herself laughing. 'Maybe I need one, too.'

'We all do at times, my dear.'

Jackie began to bark, his funny little throaty bark. Sheelagh accepted the hint, glancing at her watch.

'I had no idea it was so late. I hope I haven't kept you.'

'Been a pleasure, my dear. Just wait while I draw a map. Our roads are a real maze. Not that I've ever driven a car, but Ernie has a small truck, so we get around.'

'You must come and see me some time.'

'I'd love to, my dear. Real treat to meet a girl like you. Just a mo, I'll get a bit of paper and a pencil...'

Mrs Nucket hurried away while Sheelagh played with the little dog. Poor Luke, it must have been awful to have a wife who screamed and threw things at you. Yet he hadn't forgotten her. Sheelagh knew that.

With the map in her hand, she said goodbye to the friendly old woman and drove the short cut up the mountainside and along the winding earth tracks. It was about four o'clock when she saw her house, standing alone facing the ocean.

She parked the car under the shade of the trees and went inside, Jackie racing ahead, his little tail wagging. As Sheelagh went up the steps to the verandah she saw Luke standing in front of her easel.

'Luke, you're early,' she said.

He turned to look at her, his face hard. 'Too early?'

'Of course not. Lovely to see you. Jackie and I went exploring and met a sweet old woman. Mrs Nucket ... a real darling.'

'What made you go there?' His voice was cold.

'Chance. I felt restless, so we went for a drive and then I saw that little house with the English words: *Bed and Board,* so I went there.'

'You hurt Mercury's feelings, Sheelagh.

Why did you drive away when you saw us?'

Sheelagh's cheeks were hot. 'Why? Why – well, because I was in a bad mood and not fit to cope with Mercury. Much as I like him, you must admit he is a bit – well, over-powering.'

'Why were you in a bad mood? Bored? Lonely?'

'Of course I wasn't.' She felt her temper beginning to rise. 'I just felt I couldn't take any more, but had to, and the only way was to get out of the house and ... and get over it.'

'Over what?'

This was the Luke who had 'moods'. The one she seldom saw but who was frightening when she did. It was absurd to fight at a time like this, it could only get worse.

'Nothing. Let's forget it.' She turned away, but his hand was on her shoulder, turning her round.

'You're the one who always says we must talk about things. What upset you?'

'Nothing, really.' She looked up at him. 'I don't like telling you, because I'm ashamed. Dad always says...'

'Let's leave your dad out of this for a change. I get tired of hearing his name,' Luke said angrily. She stared at him in amazement – so she was right in what she had thought several times; Luke was as jealous of her father as she was of Gina!

She slipped out of his grasp and went to her painting. 'Isn't it ghastly? I lost my temper because it was so bad.'

Luke came to stand by her side. 'I like it. It's good.'

Startled, she turned. 'You're joking?'

'I am not. Will you give it to me? I'll have it framed and we'll hang it in the bedroom.'

'But it's ... I mean, I didn't paint it,' Sheelagh told him. 'I'd been trying to show something ... that tree over there.' She pointed it out. 'No leaves, no life, just stark branches going up into the sky as if trying to get something, and the flowers round the tree roots so beautiful and – well, I wanted to paint that, but it was a flop, so I lost my temper and flung the paint on the canvas.'

'I still like it. So it's mine?'

'Of course, if you really want it.'

'How many times do I have to tell you I really want it?' He caught hold of her arm, swinging her round to face him. 'Look, what upset you? I'm not letting go of you until you tell me.' His voice was cold and she sighed.

'All right, if you must know, I'm jealous.'

His face seemed to work as if he was trying

not to smile.

'You're jealous? Why?'

'I ... I found Gina's photograph. You said she was in the past, but you kept her photograph...'

'I haven't kept a single photograph of hers.'

'It's there.' Sheelagh pointed to the tallboy. 'You also said you got rid of all the furniture and bought new for me.'

'I did – except for one or two bits given me by the islanders. That was one. Why are you looking at me like that? You calling me a liar?'

'I'm not, but the photo is there.'

Quickly she told him about Jackie's disappearance under the tallboy, her difficulty in pulling him out, and how he brought the little package. 'I went to pick it up and the photograph came out. It could only be Gina. She was lovely.'

'I don't know how it got there. I certainly didn't put it anywhere. But what if I had? It happened a long time ago.'

'You still love her.'

He shook her so that her hair swung. 'How many times have I to tell you I don't? Where was the package?'

'On the floor. The bottom drawer is full of

160

her things.'

'It is?' He looked puzzled, let her go and strode down the verandah and into the main room, Sheelagh following him. He jerked open the bottom drawer of the tallboy and stood looking puzzled at it. Then he turned to Sheelagh, his face clearing as if a problem had been solved. 'It may have been done by Mercury. After it happened, he sent me off on a job in Paris, and when I came back, everything to do with Gina had gone.'

He bent and picked out the small bundle, looked at the photograph and tore it in half, tossed it into the waste paper basket and looked at Sheelagh. 'Satisfied?' he asked. 'I had no idea it was there.' Then he looked at the letters and frowned. 'Viola's writing – I'd know it anywhere. Waste of time to read such tripe.' He tossed them into the basket, too.

'You don't think Gina wanted you to read them? That it was why she left them here? I mean...' Sheelagh stumbled over the words because of the look on Luke's face. 'I mean, there must be some reason why she left them.'

'For crying out loud!' Luke pulled out the drawer and tipped the contents into the basket. 'Why can't you forget the whole thing, just as I've done? You harp on and on until...' he said, putting the drawer back, turning to look at her. 'A fine welcome home, I must say! Mercury sent me back because he was worried about you, and when I get here, not only are you out but when you come back you imply that I'm a liar, and now you want to dig up the past!'

He walked past her, outside, slamming the door, and in a few moments she heard the roar of his car engine as he drove past the house.

Sheelagh stood still for a few moments, then slowly, almost as if mesmerised, she went to the waste paper basket, sorting out things until she had the package of letters and the torn up photograph in her hands. She wrapped them up in paper, wondering why she was doing this yet knowing that she must. It was very strange and yet she felt much happier when she had tucked the sealed package at the back of one of her dressing-table drawers. Somehow – she could not explain how – she had a feeling that one day those letters might prove important.

Then she took the waste paper basket to the kitchen and told Tarantula to throw the rubbish away. Back in her own room, Sheelagh stood very still, her hands against her face. It was only the warm feel of Jackie's tongue on her bare legs that brought her back to where she was. She bent and picked up the little dog, resting her cheek against his soft coat.

'Sorry, Jackie, you want a walk?'

Jackie's little body throbbed with excitement, his tail wagged furiously.

'Come on,' she said, and led the way down to the long empty white beach and began to throw sticks for him.

She felt tired, even exhausted. Had she done wrong again? Should she have said nothing about Gina's photograph or the letters? If only she knew how to think before she spoke!

CHAPTER 7

Early that evening, the big white car drew up and a chauffeur got out to open the car door. Sheelagh, sitting on the verandah with Jackie on her lap, was startled, and then when she saw the huge ponderous body of Mercury slowly get out as he glanced up at her, lifting his hand in greeting, she wondered why he was there.

She went down the steps to meet the monstrosity, who had such a friendly smile these days.

'This is a surprise,' she greeted him.

His enormous hand engulfed hers, but gently. 'I had to see you, my dear, because I was worried. Have I offended you in some way?' he asked, his voice anxious. 'I mean, I know I have a queer sense of humour at times, but I didn't mean to.'

'Oh, Mercury, you didn't offend me at all,' Sheelagh said warmly. 'And I like your sense of humour. You're wondering why I didn't stop when I saw you and Luke in town? Do come up and we'll get you a cold drink.'

'With gin, my dear.'

'Of course.' She led the way up the steps, looking over shoulder, tossing back her long dark hair. 'Come on, Jackie!' she called, but the little dog had already raced by her and was waiting by her chair. 'Sit down, Mercury, while I call Tarantula.'

Later as they sat, sipping their ice-cold drinks, Mercury said slowly: 'It's no business of mine, my dear, but what made you turn and run when you saw us in town?'

'Turn and run?' Sheelagh laughed. 'You're too clever. I thought I'd done it so quickly you wouldn't see me.'

164

'What was wrong? You mad with Luke?'

'Oh no ... no. I was angry with myself.' She felt tempted to tell him the whole story, yet something stopped her. If Luke learned that she had asked Mercury if he had put Gina's photograph, letters and things in the tallboy, Luke might – in the strange mood he was in – believe she didn't think he had told her the truth, and that could start another quarrel. 'No, Mercury, it wasn't Luke's fault. It was just the way I felt. You know how at times everything seems to go wrong.'

Mercury chuckled. 'Too right I do, my girlie. Luke tells me you've done a fine picture. He was quite impressed. How about showing it to me?'

They walked down to the easel, Mercury standing back, peering at it, with his hand up. 'I like it,' he said.

Sheelagh laughed. 'You sound just as surprised as Luke did. Actually it was an accident. I made a mess of what I was trying to paint, lost my temper and flung on the paint.'

'Maybe it would be a good idea to lose your temper more often,' Mercury said, turning to look at her, a strange expression on his face that Sheelagh could not understand. 'By the way, Luke asked me to tell you he won't be home to dinner.'

'He won't?' Sheelagh knew she sounded dismayed and tried to smile. 'I should be used to it.' What really troubled her was the reason why Luke wasn't coming home. Was he still angry with her? How complicated marriage was, she thought, so very different from what you expect it to be.

'I wondered if you'd do me the honour to come out to dinner with me,' Mercury went on.

'Why not stay here and dine with me?' Sheelagh suggested. 'I know Tarantula has cooked a good meal.'

They walked back to their chairs. 'Nothing would delight me more, lass, if you're sure Luke won't be jealous? I mean, I might try to seduce you.' His one good eye was twinkling as he stared at her, but Sheelagh had a hard battle to keep from bursting out laughing, for who on earth would be seduced by this Humpty Dumpty of a man, nice as he was?

'No. You're his best friend.'

'Am I? That's good to hear. When you're a success, you make so many enemies on the way. What on earth's that?' Mercury pointed at Jackie as if seeing him for the first time.

'That's my Jackie.' Sheelagh stroked the

little dog with the big ears and ever-wagging tail.

'*Your* dog?' Mercury echoed, his voice odd, and Sheelagh felt her cheeks burning. She knew what Mercury meant – she should have said *our* dog. She could feel Mercury's disapproval.

'Well,' she said defiantly, 'Luke is so seldom at home these days that Jackie hardly knows him.'

Mercury nodded as if he understood. 'I know, dear. We're going through a bad spell. Things'll quieten down later.'

Tarantula rang the jangling bell, so they went into the dining-room end of the long room. Mercury looked round approvingly.

'You liked the furniture Luke chose for you?'

'Very much, but we're going to repaint the walls and I want to make some new curtains and ... and...' Sheelagh began, and laughed. 'I don't know why, but somehow we never get round to doing it.'

'Why not organise it yourself? Have you met Ernie Nucket? You haven't?'

'I met his wife. She's nice.'

'A good couple. Well, you contact Ernie and he'll get you half a dozen boys to come and paint.'

'But Luke...' Sheelagh hesitated, not wanting to say too much.

'I doubt if he'll even notice it. You're the one that lives here, anyhow. You go ahead.'

She smiled. 'Right. By the way, I'm getting on with those manuscripts you gave me. Do you honestly think there could be treasure here in sunken vessels?'

'I can see Martha Nucket's been talking! I doubt it, but there's always the chance. Ernie heard of it years ago, that's how they got here. When those MSS. came into my hands, I thought maybe there was some truth. Anyhow, how are you doing?'

They discussed the manuscripts, the difficulty sometimes in translating what was obviously not pure French, but that she found it interesting.

They were back in their chairs with coffee on the table by their side again when Luke returned. He went straight to Sheelagh and kissed her so that she felt some of the tension leaving her, then handed her a handful of letters.

'Thanks,' she said, turning the letters over. Several were from her friends at home, but the one she opened quickly while Luke and Mercury talked was the letter from her father.

She read it once. She read it twice, and even again, then folded the letter up and put it away in the envelope, her face troubled.

She opened the other letters and tried to look interested, but the words in her father's letter went round and round in her head.

Much later when Mercury had gone to his own house and Tarantula was finished, Luke followed Sheelagh into the bedroom and put his hand on her shoulder, turning her round.

'What's wrong? Was it your father's letter?'

Sheelagh nodded. 'Viola Whittaker has been to see them.'

'What?' Luke almost shouted. 'Why, the... Look, what did she tell them? About the terrible life you're suffering, what a monster I am? No, she can't have told him that or else darling daddy would have been on the first plane out here to slaughter me.'

'Please, Luke, don't make it worse. I don't know what Viola said, and Dad wrote very carefully. He doesn't actually say *anything*, but I can read between the lines that that hateful woman has said something to upset him but that he knows it isn't his affair and... Oh, Luke, why does she have to mess up everything?'

'Because she's made that way, I suppose,'

169

Luke said with a shrug.

'Luke, you don't think she'll tell Zoe lies?'

'Zoe? Where does she come into this?'

'I don't know, but I'm frightened. Zoe is your daughter, Luke, but Viola is capable of telling her awful lies about you.'

'Would it matter?'

'Of course it would. Don't you want your daughter to love you?' Sheelagh was shocked.

Luke put his arms round her. 'Of course I do, but I don't think Mrs Hamilton would let Viola near the girl.' He sat down on the bed, pulling Sheelagh close, stroking her hair gently. 'You see, Mrs Hamilton never liked Viola. It began when Gina first went to boarding school. She was a frightened kid and Viola, eight years older and a prefect, took Gina under her wing. Gina was always grateful for this and had an absolute crush – you know what school kids are like. She used to ask Viola back for the holidays and the friendship lasted. That was how it all began. Mrs Hamilton made it plain she didn't like Viola, but, as so often happens, the more Gina's mother ran down Viola, the more Gina clung to her. Gina always believed every word Viola said. She was her shadow, too, writing long letters every week, asking her advice about everything.

'Except about you?'

Luke bent and kissed Sheelagh's neck. 'Exactly. Did you consult your best friend about me?'

'Most certainly not!' Sheelagh turned her head so that her mouth met his. 'I loved you – I knew it, and that was all.'

'Gina didn't love me. This was the puzzling part of it. Viola was against the marriage, yet I'm sure she told Gina I was Mercury's heir. It was as if she wanted to smash the marriage before it began. Anyhow, Gina was very upset because Viola behaved badly at the reception. Frankly, I think Viola's pride was hurt. Gina had put her on top of a pedestal and Viola wanted to stay up there.'

'Instead you were up there?'

'Not for long,' he said, his voice suddenly tired. 'She told me plainly that she'd married me because she thought I was rich.'

Sheelagh's arms went round him. 'Well, I didn't. I never even thought of it. I married you because I loved you.'

'Precisely,' Luke laughed, but even as he held her close and kissed her, Sheelagh had the uncomfortable feeling that Luke had loved Gina far more than he admitted, or perhaps realised. She stifled a sigh – Gina had been dead for years. It was crazy to be jealous of a dead woman. Somehow, Sheelagh knew, she must find a way to kill her jealousy.

Taking Mercury's advice, Sheelagh asked Luke if it was okay for her to get Ernie Nucket to find some locals to paint the house for her. He looked startled.

'Of course. Sorry, I'd forgotten all about it. We did decide what colours, didn't we?' he asked.

'Yes. I'd like to meet Ernie, I thought of asking them to a meal.'

'By all means,' Luke smiled. 'But not when I'm around. They're both good people, but their gratitude for the small things I've done for them, I find embarrassing,' he admitted.

'They think you're super,' Sheelagh teased.

'Don't you?' Luke laughed across the dinner table.

'No,' she said, tossing back her hair, her eyes shining. 'I think you're super-super.'

'That's my girl!' grinned Luke. His face grew grave. 'Everything is all right? I mean, you're not bored?'

'Bored?' Sheelagh laughed as she led the way back to the verandah and the waiting coffee. 'I never have time – what with Jackie, the garden, my painting, the manuscripts.'

'Incidentally, Mercury is very impressed by you,' Luke told her, stretching out his long legs and relaxing in his chair. 'You get on well.'

'I can't help it. There's something about him...'

Luke moved swiftly, scooped her up in his arms and sat down again, holding her close to him. 'There's something about you, my little one,' he said, kissing her.

As the days passed, Sheelagh was so happy that sometimes she was almost afraid. It seemed too good to be true. Ernie and Martha Nucket had lunched with her. Ernie, a little wizened man with a few wisps of hair and bright blue eyes, a sun-tanned skin and an enormous energy, had beamed at the idea of painting the house.

'Just leave it to me. I'll bring along the colour sheet so you can choose the paint.'

'You have to get that from Moroni?'

'Yes, but that's no problem with our daily boat. In the past it was different.'

Mrs Nucket made a great fuss of Jackie. 'If you ever go away with Luke,' she said, 'leave the little lad with me. I'm fond of dogs, but

Ernie here, he's allergic to them. Or so he says!'

Ernie chuckled. 'I'm just jealous. I like my woman to have only one man, and that's me.'

'Ernie!' Martha pretended to be shocked.

'That's awfully good of you,' said Sheelagh. 'Luke has talked of us flying over to New York one day and ... well, Tarantula is very good, but I'm afraid Jackie doesn't like her.'

The little black dog with his enormous flapping ears and tail that never seemed to be still was lying on his back, legs in the air, while Martha tickled him.

'He obviously likes you,' Sheelagh smiled. That was another problem solved, she thought happily.

So the locals came and the house was a shambles with Tarantula tripping around, finding things this time to fall over as well as the imaginary ones she usually did. Her apron seemed to slide down several times a day and she was forever scolding the painters.

'The mess they make!' she complained in French to Sheelagh.

'*C'est la vie*,' Sheelagh shrugged, and Tarantula went off in a burst of laughter, repeating the words and almost choking with amusement.

'*C'est la vie … c'est la vie!*'

The house certainly looked much better with the fresh paint in the colours they had chosen; then Sheelagh got to work on the curtains. Luckily Martha had a sewing machine which she lent her; also at the store in town there was quite a lot of brightly coloured material.

Luke was in a good mood, coming home much more often to meals, and Sheelagh had written a long letter to her father, telling him how happy she was, describing the Nuckets, the lovely beach, the huge waves that pounded noisily but that after a while, you didn't even hear, so accustomed to them you got; about Jackie, the garden that wasn't too good but they were rather short of water, the curtains she was making. She made it a long letter, trying to give him some idea of her life and showing, without mentioning Viola, that it was a full, happy one. She wrote about the palm trees, the huge bushes covered with creamy-white fragrant flowers, the brightly coloured birds that were always flying around, the odd little animals you saw if you ventured into clumps of trees.

'It's funny, but there never seems time to do everything,' she finished her letter. 'Each day is really too short. I'm looking forward to your visit and do hope my garden will look better then.'

So the days passed, and then one evening, Luke came home early, his face grave. He tossed a letter to her.

'Read it while I have a shower and then I'll get us drinks. It's been quite a day and this is the last straw!'

Sheelagh drew the letter out of the envelope.

'Dear Luke,' she read. Puzzled, she turned to the last page and the signature. *Rene Hamilton*. It could only be Gina's mother.

Sheelagh read on. It was a sad but bravely written letter in which Mrs Hamilton said her husband had died suddenly. 'I'm afraid the time has come for me to part with Zoe, Luke. It will break my heart, because we love her so much and it has made such a difference to our lives since Gina died. Unfortunately I'm getting bad attacks of arthritis, perhaps because my Reg has been ill for some time, though only he and I knew it. No longer can I cope with a house of this size, so I plan to sell it and move into an old people's home or a residential hotel if I can find one I can afford. The heavy taxes take a lot off one, unfortunately.

176

'Zoe is now nearly eleven, a bright girl, friendly, not very good at school, but that's largely laziness, I think. Gina was just the same. Zoe knows about you, that you live on a lonely island and we had all felt it would be better for her to stay in England with us. She also knows you are the generous Uncle L. who sent her the lovely presents. I wouldn't have made this decision, Luke, but I've just heard you have married again, so quite a few of your problems are solved. Zoe should now be in a normal household with a father and mother. I'm not rushing things, but perhaps next time you're in England, you would come in and see me so that we can make a plan.'

Sheelagh had just finished when Luke came in, wearing a brief pair of shorts, his hair and body still damp from the cold shower.

'Well?' he said.

Looking up, Sheelagh saw the strain on his face.

'Poor Mrs Hamilton,' she said. 'Of course Zoe must come here.'

He filled two glasses with ice-cold drinks and then came to sit near her. 'There's no *of course* about it. Personally I think a boarding school is the answer.'

177

'Not so soon, Luke. She's just lost her grandfather and then her grandmother. Give her time!'

He looked surprised. 'You think so? Actually I see what Mrs Hamilton means. Their house is very big. It always was a problem as regards domestic help, and their garden ... well, luckily Gina's father was a keen gardener and a healthy man. I had no idea he was ill. I wish I had,' he said thoughtfully. 'I hate the idea of her going into an old folks' home. She's a typical English countrywoman – tweeds and her hair plaited round her head, if you get me.'

'It must be hard to give up your home after so many years. Luke,' Sheelagh hesitated, but only for a moment. 'Why not let's ask both Zoe and Mrs Hamilton to come out here? It would cheer Mrs Hamilton up and also make it easier for Zoe, meeting a strange father and stepmother, if she has her grannie with her.'

'You're being very noble. You wouldn't mind them coming here?'

'I'd love it.' Sheelagh leaned forward eagerly. 'Zoe is your daughter, Luke, so I'll love her and she'll be mine, too. I've always wanted children.'

A cloud seemed to close over Luke's face.

'In other words you want a child and I've failed to give you one.'

Sheelagh caught her breath. Why had he to misunderstand everything she said and twist it to mean something else?

'I didn't say that, nor did I mean it,' she said quickly. 'After all, we haven't been married long and...'

'You're wondering if I can, so you'd like Zoe in case I can't?'

'Luke, please ... please don't go off in one of your moods. You know very well I've always been worried about Zoe and wanted her to live with us. It has nothing to do with you being able to give me a child, you know that. You're just being difficult, and please don't!'

Luke stared at her for a moment, then moved with his swift grace to kneel by her side, putting his arms round her loosely, linking them with his hands. 'You're right, darling, and I'm sorry, but things are very tough at the moment. We've got four Yankees coming over to discuss future development on some of the islands and they'll stay at Mercury's house, but I'll have to cope with them. He's gone off to Japan for some reason that made him very excited, but he won't tell me. This would happen now! I don't see how

I can go.'

'Let me go, then. I can talk to Mrs Hamilton and persuade her to come out with the child for a holiday.'

He let go of her, his hands falling away as he sat back on his heels, his eyes narrowing. 'Is it just an excuse to call and see darling daddy?' he asked.

Her hand moved faster than her thoughts: there was a crisp slapping sound and she found herself staring at Luke, her hand pressed against her mouth, her eyes wide with dismay, as he gingerly touched his red cheek. Then she jumped up. 'You know that's not true! I love Dad, but I love you quite differently. If you had any sense you'd know that!' She turned away, suddenly in despair. Was life always going to be like this? Short happy times and then Luke being so difficult, so unlike himself?

He caught hold of her. 'I know. I'm a swine and a heel, but I happen to love you, that's why I'm jealous. Okay, you're right, love,' he said, and his voice was tender again. 'You go over and see Mrs Hamilton and bring them both back with you. Right?' he asked, his mouth close to hers.

'Right,' she began to say, but the word vanished as he kissed her.

CHAPTER 8

Sheelagh's father was waiting for her at Heathrow. As he came forward to greet her, the past six months seemed to fall away like a cape she had tossed off, and she ran into his arms. She was shocked to see how much older he looked, his hair was whiter, and his smile was stiff as if forced.

He led the way to his car. 'Your mother sends her love and will have your favourite meal ready,' he promised.

Sitting by his side as they went through the London traffic, Sheelagh kept looking at him worriedly. This was no time to talk to him, she felt, for his questions were obviously studied carefully, as if he was afraid of the answers.

'I've got some lovely snaps, even some of my little Jackie,' she told him.

'You have? Good. We'd like to see them,' he said, his voice sad. Sheelagh felt a surge of fury rush through her. Viola must have upset her father. Would that hateful woman never leave them alone?

181

It was not until they were out of London's traffic and on the wide straight roads leading to the south coast that she turned to him.

'I expect you're wondering why I've come home?'

He looked uncomfortable. 'Well, it was so sudden.'

'I know. Luke's very efficient. He would have come, but he's up to his eyes in work. Actually I've come over to fetch his daughter.'

She saw the way his hands tensed on the steering wheel. 'You know, then?'

'Oh, Dad darling, we've so much to talk about. I suppose that beastly woman, Viola, has told you a lot of lies.'

'I certainly hope so. Look, Sheelagh love, let's not talk about it now, because your mother is as worried as I am about you and you can tell us both what went wrong.'

'Went wrong?' Sheelagh was really startled. 'Nothing has gone wrong, Dad. I love Luke very much and he loves me. It's simply that his father-in-law, I mean by his first marriage, has died, and Mrs Hamilton wants us to have Zoe. I'm very glad about it.'

He looked at her quickly. 'Tell us all about it later.' He sounded tired and unhappy, and

Sheelagh's fury for Viola grew.

October was a beautiful month, she thought, as she looked at the trees, their leaves a glorious gold or red. It was warm too, but cold in the evenings, and so that night, after a meal with her mother and father, they sat round the fire.

Her mother, too, looked worried. She kept beginning to speak and then closed her mouth again as if deciding to say nothing, Sheelagh saw.

Sheelagh stood up before the fire and looked at them. 'Please tell me what lies that hateful woman told you?' she burst out. 'First, I'm going to tell you that there's nothing wrong with our marriage. Luke and I are as much in love as we were before. Does that help?'

She saw her mother's eyes blinking as she nodded, and Sheelagh's father smiled.

'Yes, that helps a lot, Sheelagh dear. When we got your cable saying when you were arriving, we both remembered what Miss Whittaker had told us.'

'I knew she'd said something from the guarded way you wrote, Dad.'

'She told us all about the first marriage ... and that you knew nothing when you married Luke. Is that right?'

'Quite right. Viola told me as I waited in the chancel. Remember how worried about me you were, Dad?'

He frowned. 'She told you then?'

'Yes. She said I was much prettier than his first wife.'

'Luke hadn't told you he'd been married before,' Sheelagh's mother said, her voice disapproving.

'I think he thought I knew. He said it was of no importance – that the past was best forgotten.'

'I agree,' said her father. 'All the same, it must have been a shock to you. No wonder you looked white as a sheet.'

'And that wasn't all, Dad. When I was changing to leave the reception, she caught me. Just before you came along. She told me Luke had killed his first wife and would kill me in the same way.' Sheelagh heard her mother's horrified gasp, but went on, 'She also told me he had a daughter he had deserted.'

'Yes, she told us that,' her father said. 'I didn't believe her about the killing part, but I was rather shocked about the deserted child.'

'So was I,' her mother put in quickly.

Sheelagh laughed. 'So was I,' she ad-

184

mitted. 'We had quite a row about it, but...'
Then she told them what Luke had said,
how the marriage had never been a success,
how Viola had influenced Gina, how Gina
had left him, never telling him a child was
on the way. 'When Gina died, her mother
wrote and asked Luke to let them keep the
baby. Zoe was eighteen months old. Luke
lived on this primitive island...'

'So it is primitive?' her father asked quickly.

'Not nowadays. It might have been then,
Dad. Anyhow, Luke lived alone, was always
being sent by Mercury all over the world.'

'Mercury? Who on earth is that?' her
father demanded.

'I can't remember his name. I think... No,
I'll probably remember it later, but he had
some trouble with mercury as a boy in
science class and that was his nickname. He
and Luke are partners. Anyhow, Mrs
Hamilton begged Luke to let her have Zoe,
she promised that when the child was old
enough, she could go back to her father.
Luke used to send her presents as Uncle L.
He also saw her at school and paid everything for her.'

'That's a different story from Viola's,'
Sheelagh's father said grimly.

'I know. But I'd rather believe Luke than

Viola Whittaker, Dad. Besides, Mercury...
Oh, I've got it! His name is James William
Potter.'

'Not *the* Potter?' her father sounded
impressed.

'Yes. Luke has worked for him for years.
Now they're partners. I see quite a lot of him
when he comes to the island.' She began to
laugh and couldn't stop. When they asked
her what was funny, she tried to describe
Mercury. 'He's sort of square, as big as he's
short.' She used her hands to demonstrate
the size of his paunch, then remembered
how Tarantula had described him, and
laughed as she told them of Tarantula's
habits of stumbling and also losing her
apron. 'But she cooks well and the house is
always clean.'

'It seems funny to think of you as a house-
wife,' Sheelagh's father said.

Sheelagh laughed. 'It was funny at first,
but now I don't even notice it.'

'But you're happy?' asked her mother.
'That's the main thing.'

'I'm very happy,' Sheelagh agreed, and
wondered if she had said it too firmly. 'Of
course it isn't all honey and roses, Mum. We
quarrel and he's out a lot, but most of the
time we're very happy. If only that woman

would leave us alone! She's hated Luke for years,' Sheelagh went on, telling them how Luke had first met the Whittakers, about Viola's visit to the island when Luke was away. 'Luke never found out why Gina left him. Maybe her mother will tell us. We're asking her out to stay, as her husband's just died.' Sheelagh told them of the letter Luke had received. 'I suggested we ask her out as it would be easier for Zoe to adapt herself if her grandmother was there.'

'A good idea, Sheelagh. It won't be easy for this child to accept a stepmother as well as a father she's never seen.'

'I'm only hoping this Viola Whittaker hasn't said nasty things to Zoe,' Sheelagh sighed.

Her mother stood up hastily, her face anxious. 'I wish you'd told us about this awful woman so that we'd have been on guard when she came. I'll make us some coffee – or would you prefer chocolate, Sheelagh?'

'Coffee, please.'

Her father laughed. 'You have grown up!' When they were alone, he said, 'This Whittaker woman could be a real menace. She talked mostly to your mother, who was terribly upset. She wanted me to fly out to rescue you.' He gave an odd laugh.

'I don't need rescuing, Dad. I'm very

happy, honestly I am. Now I'll go and get those snaps, because tomorrow I must go up to Esher to see Mrs Hamilton.' She ran upstairs and brought back the snaps.

They certainly impressed her mother and father, especially Mercury's house.

'I prefer ours,' Sheelagh told them. 'His is too – well, melodramatic. His wife hates it. I've not discovered why, yet.'

'He must be very rich,' her mother commented.

Sheelagh's father frowned. 'Of course he is. He's a millionaire.'

Sheelagh and her father drove to Esher the next day. The house was large, obviously several centuries old and just outside Esher.

As her father stopped the car, he turned to look at her.

'You really are happy?' he asked.

She smiled. 'Really, truly, Dad. Look, you've been married much longer than me and you know that ... well, one doesn't always agree and ... well, sometimes things go wrong, but isn't that absolutely normal?'

It was his turn to smile. 'You've soon learned!'

'Well, Luke is having a tough time. He's working hard, they have problems, and as he told me, he gets frightfully frustrated, and when he comes home...'

'Blows his top,' her father finished for her. 'I'm afraid I do, too. But if things don't go right, you promise to let me know?'

Sheelagh put her hand over his. 'I promise, Dad,' she said, and added silently: *If there is anything you can do to help us.* There was no point in worrying him if there wasn't.

'All right, then, love. I'll pick you up some time about five?'

'Lovely, Dad,' she said, and got out of the car, turning to watch him drive away. That hateful Viola Whittaker, Sheelagh thought, why had she to go round spilling acid into other people's emotional lives?

Sheelagh looked up at the big square house covered with ivy and the neat front garden with its curved path and the lawn covered with leaves that were falling all the time. As she walked to the front door, she wondered what Gina's mother would be like. Luke had liked her, but...

The front door opened and a tall, very thin woman came out. She looked tired, her eyes red-rimmed as if many tears had been shed, but she held out her hand.

'You must be Luke's wife. I saw the car draw up ... was that your father?'

'Yes. He has to go to London on business, so dropped me off. He'll pick me up this afternoon.'

'I hoped you'd stay for a few nights and give Zoe a chance to know you. Do come in.'

As they walked up the six stone steps and into the cold hall, Sheelagh explained, 'I've come just to talk it over with you, Mrs Hamilton. Luke will make all the arrangements. I haven't seen Dad and Mum for over six months and I wouldn't dare suggest sleeping anywhere other than at home.'

The tall thin woman with greying hair and lines either side of her mouth smiled. 'I understand. It is good of you to come over. I've some coffee ready.'

'Thanks.' Sheelagh looked around at the antique furniture, the dark curtains, the large rooms. As Mrs Hamilton had said, this was too big a house for a lone woman.

The kitchen was large but more cheerful than the rest of the house and they sat at the table talking. 'I've wanted to move for years,' Mrs Hamilton admitted, 'but my husband, Reg, loved it because it was his grandfather's house. I always found it difficult to get any domestic help, but Reg was very good at helping. You're much younger than I expected,' Mrs Hamilton finished abruptly, her pale blue eyes narrowing as she looked at Sheelagh.

'Everyone says that, but I'm not so young, really,' Sheelagh said. 'I'm nearly twenty-one.'

Mrs Hamilton laughed. 'That's quite an age, my dear. You're sure you don't mind having Zoe?'

'I'll love having her. Ever since I knew Luke had a daughter I wanted her to come and live with us, but Luke explained the situation and ... well, to be honest, I love my own father very much and I felt Zoe *should* have a father, but when Luke told me about you and your husband, I agreed that it wouldn't be fair to take her away. She must be very upset at the moment.'

'Upset? You mean about my husband? Yes, very, but she's a strange girl, she sort of retreats and locks her lips. She's thrilled at the thought of meeting her father.'

'We wondered if you'd come out to the island with her and...' Sheelagh said.

'Me?' Mrs Hamilton looked startled. 'But I've never been out of England. I'm too old to start travelling now.'

'I think you'd like it, but actually I ... we were thinking of Zoe. I mean...' Sheelagh hesitated. 'She's lost her grandfather, got a stranger for a father – and worse still, there's me.'

Mrs Hamilton rose and refilled the cups with coffee.

'You've a point there, but all the same...' She looked round her worriedly. 'It's quite a thought. You know, my husband and I, we ... well, we sort of clung to the past and what was familiar. We were so worried when Gina went out to stay with Viola.' She hesitated for a moment, her eyes worried as she looked at her son-in-law's new wife. 'You have met Viola?'

'I most certainly have,' Sheelagh said with a new grimness. 'She did her best to wreck our marriage before it had taken place.'

'She did?' Mrs Hamilton sounded shocked. 'She did a lot of harm to Gina, too, yet Gina loved her dearly. We couldn't understand it at all. Well, when poor Gina had an unhappy love affair and the invitation came, we were against it, but Gina wanted to go, and...' Mrs Hamilton shrugged, 'when Gina wanted something... Then when she wrote to say she was marrying and going to be living out there for a short while ... well, we had to put up with it. It was very sad the way the marriage collapsed. She came home so frightened.'

'Frightened?' Sheelagh was puzzled.

At that moment there was a ring at the back door and Mrs Hamilton went to answer it. Sheelagh looked round her. How clean it was! What a lot of work must be involved. There were two things Mrs Hamilton had said that puzzled Sheelagh. Why had Gina said she was going to live on the island for 'a short while'? The way Luke had spoken, it had seemed he had a permanent job there. And why had Gina been very *frightened* when she came home?

'Come upstairs, dear,' Mrs Hamilton was saying as she brought in some bread that had been delivered. 'I've some snaps to show you. Gina was a beautiful girl, but she was spoilt – our fault, for she was our only child. She always wanted her own way and usually got it. I'm afraid Zoe is much the same. I ... I hope she won't be a nuisance?'

'I'm sure she won't be,' Sheelagh said as she followed her hostess upstairs to a small sitting-room facing the front. 'And Luke won't stand any nonsense.'

'Tantrums are funny things. Zoe gets them at times – just screams and bangs things. Reg – that's my ... I mean that was my husband ... he had a perfect answer. He just roared with laughter and that usually got Zoe laughing too. I'm afraid I'm not so successful. Look, here are some snaps. This was Gina as a baby, wasn't she cute...?'

For the next hour or more, Sheelagh sat by Mrs Hamilton's side, looking at the various snaps of Gina, and thinking more and more that Gina must have been far more beautiful than Luke had admitted. Had he deliberately failed to say she was? She saw pictures of Gina at different ages right up until her wedding-day, then no photographs at all until several years later when there were some of Gina with her baby. There were plenty of Zoe, of course, who was amazingly like her mother.

Mrs Hamilton suddenly remembered lunch. 'My dear, I am sorry, talking all the time like this!' She led the way to the kitchen and produced a tin of salmon and a tin of asparagus.

'I'm afraid I'm in a bit of a daze half the time. I forget all about food,' she admitted as she opened the tins. 'When I got Luke's cable I didn't know whether to cry or be pleased. You see, it means a complete ... well, a complete upheaval in my life. After years of marriage and motherhood, it's going to be terribly different, yet my doctor says I must. That I'm getting too tired.'

'Then please think about coming to stay with us for a while,' Sheelagh urged.

Mrs Hamilton shook her head. 'I'm too old to go to a new land. After all, I have friends here ... or,' she added rather bitterly, 'I thought I had.'

'When does Zoe come home from school?'

'About four o'clock. She gets a lift back with a friend. That's another thing that's worrying me. What about her education? She's like Gina, not very bright and bored with it all, but every girl should know how to earn her own living, because you never can tell.'

'Luke suggested boarding school, but ... well, I thought it would be rather much for Zoe, everything happening at once,' said Sheelagh. 'I never went to boarding school, but I should think it's pretty awful after always living at home.'

'I went and was very much happier than when at home,' Mrs Hamilton admitted with a smile. 'I was the middle child, you see. Isn't there a school or schools on the island?'

'Yes, there are several. Or for a year, perhaps we could teach her at home by a correspondence course.' Sheelagh frowned. 'Anyhow, we'll see how things go. Luke will know what to do.'

'You love Luke very much.' It was not a question but a statement, and Sheelagh's cheeks were hot.

'Very much,' she admitted.

'I'm glad. I'm very fond of Luke and still can't understand what went wrong with him and Gina. He's been very good about Zoe. I shall miss her.' She sighed and stood up. 'I've got some jelly ... it's Zoe's favourite food!' Mrs Hamilton turned. 'Would it help if I wrote down a list of Zoe's favourite foods? And her hobbies and ... and things she hates?' she asked eagerly.

'It would be a great help. Please do,' Sheelagh said warmly, her heart full of sympathy for the old lady who so obviously feared for her grandchild, whom she was going to miss so much.

The afternoon flashed by as they discussed Zoe and her past ailments and her idiosyncrasies. Sheelagh began to feel she knew Zoe better than anyone she had ever met, yet she had not even set eyes on the girl as yet.

Then they heard the sound of a car outside. Mrs Hamilton was on her feet, nearly stumbling as she hurried to the front door. Sheelagh hesitated. How was she to greet her stepdaughter? Perhaps the wrong action might spoil everything. It couldn't be easy to suddenly have a stepmother plus a father you had never seen.

She could hear a shrill voice talking and Mrs Hamilton's softer one and then they came into the kitchen where Mrs Hamilton had just made some tea. Zoe came first – a thin, tall girl with short, curly blonde hair, and a fringe. She stared at Sheelagh, her eyes cold.

'Who are you? What's she doing here, Gran?' she asked, turning to the old woman by her side.

'She's Daddy's new wife. She's going to be your mother.'

'She can't be Daddy's wife,' Zoe said scornfully. 'My mummy was Daddy's wife.'

'But your mummy isn't here, and Daddy was lonely, so...' Mrs Hamilton said placatingly.

'I don't want a mummy! I want Daddy and you, Gran,' Zoe said, turning to her grandmother, her arms round her and beginning to scream. 'I don't want a mummy! I don't want a mummy!'

Sheelagh wished with all her heart that Luke was there to take part in the scene, for she didn't know what to do. All her sympathy was with Zoe and her grandmother. Suddenly remembering what Mrs Hamilton had said about her husband, Sheelagh thought of something. She opened her handbag and drew out the snaps.

'Like to see your new home, Zoe?' she asked. 'There are lovely white sands and coconut trees and we have a little dog. Here's the house.' She held out one snap.

Zoe, amazingly like a small child who immediately stops wailing when his interest is diverted, turned to look at it.

'It isn't very big,' she commented. Then she looked at the snaps of the little dog. 'He's nice. What's his name?'

Sheelagh told her, showed her the snaps of the garden, of the two pointed mountains that stood above the town. Then she looked at Mrs Hamilton. 'Please think about Luke's invitation, Mrs Hamilton. I think it would help a lot.'

'What invitation?' Zoe asked.

'Your daddy wants you to come out to live with us and to bring Granny, too. She needs a holiday.'

Zoe frowned. 'Of course she must come. I won't go if she doesn't.'

Sheelagh looked at Mrs Hamilton, who gave a little shrug. Looking at her watch,

Sheelagh saw her father would soon be there. So they must make plans.

'Perhaps you could close up the house – and fly out,' she suggested.

'I've never flown.'

'Nor have I,' Zoe said excitedly. 'We must fly, Granny.'

'Let Luke know what date you can come and he'll fix up everything and send you the tickets.'

'I'll...' Mrs Hamilton began, and the front door bell rang. 'I'll go,' she said, leaving Sheelagh alone with her stepdaughter for the first time.

Zoe's eyes were accusing. 'Why did you marry my daddy?' she asked.

'Because I love him.'

'I love him. He's mine, not yours. I wish you weren't going to be there!' Zoe said, as Mrs Hamilton opened the door and came in, followed by Sheelagh's father.

'I'm sorry we can't stay. It's good of you,' he was saying, 'but the traffic's pretty bad and I don't want us to be late home or my wife worries.' He smiled at Sheelagh. 'Everything organised, darling?'

Sheelagh stifled a sigh. 'I think so. Goodbye,' she said to Mrs Hamilton and Zoe, who immediately turned her back.

Following her father out to the car, Sheelagh wondered how it would work out.
Would Zoe ever accept her? Who could
blame her if she didn't?

CHAPTER 9

'You took long enough to get back,' were the
words with which Luke greeted Sheelagh on
her return to the island.

She laughed. 'I've only been gone five
days.'

'It seems like an eternity,' he said as he
took her in his arms.

He had met her at the airport at Moroni
and as they sat in the car and were driven to
the jetty where the freight ship was loading
up, he asked her how she had got on.

'Mrs Hamilton was very nice, but I'm not
sure she'll come out. Zoe wants her to.'

'Ah, Zoe. How did you get on with her?'

'I didn't, I'm afraid,' Sheelagh admitted.
'Actually I hardly saw her.'

As she told Luke about her visit to Mrs
Hamilton and the arrival of Zoe, Sheelagh
was tempted to say how much more beau-

tiful Gina had been than he ever admitted as well as such questions as 'Why didn't you tell me you both played tennis? Is it because you know I don't?' or 'You really loved her, didn't you? Your wedding photos showed me that,' but she made a great effort and managed not to let these unhappy thoughts pour out in words, for Luke was in such a good mood that she didn't want to say anything that might start off trouble.

'Zoe'll have to learn to accept you,' Luke said as they went on to the freight ship. 'You're my wife.'

Sheelagh smiled up at him, her hand tight in his.

'Darling, she's very young. We must make allowances. After all, she's lost her grandfather, is going to live in a strange place, with a father she has never known and a stepmother she thinks has stolen her mother's place.'

'We'll be patient,' he agreed, 'but I'll not have you made unhappy.'

He gave her such a sweet smile that she closed her eyes, trying to etch it on her mind so that she could always remember it.

'I hope Mrs Hamilton does come out,' Sheelagh said, 'because it would help Zoe to settle down. What about her schooling?'

'I've seen to that. For some time I've been planning to get another teacher. We have old Reamer who is quite good for the small ones, but now I've engaged an English girl who's coming out for six months or so. She's been ill and this is her solution as well as mine.'

'You've met her?'

'No – but one man in our London branch has. He says she's young, dedicated and needs a holiday badly. She'll only have about six pupils, so it shouldn't be too bad. Most of the older children here go to boarding schools.'

'How did you arrange it all in such a short time?'

'I phoned them.'

'Why didn't you phone me?'

He smiled. 'Why deny darling daddy the chance to have his little girl all to himself for a couple of days? I was afraid they'd keep you for a couple of weeks.'

'I think they'd like to, but I wanted to come back.'

'Honestly?' The ship was rolling, the huge waves outside the lagoon tossing the ship high as well. Luke put his hands on her shoulders and looked down at her. 'You really mean that? Going back to civilisation hasn't made you want to stay there?'

202

She was surprised at the ill-concealed anxiety in his voice as his hands slid down her arms.

'No, darling,' she said. 'Actually it made me realise just how much fuller a life I have out here. Dad and Mum's life is unutterably boring, doing the same thing day after day. They've aged a lot ... or so I thought.'

'They wondered why you'd gone back?'

Sheelagh laughed. 'Yes, poor darlings. They thought I'd left you.' She moved closer to him, resting her head against him, holding his hand against her cheek. 'I soon put them right and now both of them are much relieved as they're convinced I love you and am happy.'

'You really are?' he asked.

'Oh, Luke, stop being funny! You know I am.' She looked up at him and he stooped to kiss her.

'Jackie's at home, waiting for you,' he told her. 'Ernie Nucket brought him round this morning. He's organising some building for me.'

'Building?'

'Of course. We're building on two bed-rooms, a bathroom and a playroom for Zoe.'

'I hadn't thought of that,' Sheelagh confessed.

'Good thing one of us is practical,' Luke teased. 'What do you really think? That Mrs Hamilton will come out with Zoe?'

Sheelagh nodded, remembering, but deciding not to say anything about Zoe's 'tantrums'. If Zoe had made up her mind that she wanted her grandmother to come out, then Sheelagh was almost certain Mrs Hamilton would come, too. It would make everything easier!

But would it? This question was to come up to disturb Sheelagh in the weeks ahead. Somehow everything changed. Maybe it was the constant noise of the locals who were building under Ernie's direction, for Ernie's voice was to be heard shouting at them, and their laughter and shouts to one another followed so that there was never a moment of quietness during the day; maybe it was Luke's insistence that she went with him to Moroni to get furniture.

'You should know better than me what a girl of ten would like,' he said. He was joking, she knew, but she still had the uncomfortable feeling that he linked her with his daughter, that he felt the age-gap mattered more than they had thought it would.

Sheelagh said nothing, but she knew that

whatever she chose, Zoe would, on principle, hate. Somehow she must keep Zoe from knowing who chose the gay green and pink curtains, the matching rugs, and bedspread. The room for Mrs Hamilton's visit was furnished to suit any visitor.

Maybe it was also because of the feeling of tension she had, as the weeks passed and the rains came – great sheets of grey, blinding rain that made her feel more depressed than ever.

Why she felt so depressed, she could not tell, but one wet afternoon when the builders had taken refuge from the heavy rain and Jackie was curled up on her lap, Sheelagh tried to face up to facts.

Why was she depressed? Because of the weather? Surely not, for Luke had assured her the rainy season only lasted a few months. Because of Luke? Definitely not, for he was in a very good mood, loving, attentive, home every night for dinner, as this was not the busy season at the hotels on the islands. Because of what? It was that strange feeling she sometimes got of a big black cloud moving overhead and into her life, as if she was waiting for something to happen, something she could not stop.

Her immediate relief, when a letter came

from Mrs Hamilton saying she had decided to stay on in her house until the New Year and was then letting it furnished to some very nice friends, and that she thought it was better for Zoe to stay at school till the end of term, also that might be better for them to have Christmas in England with all their friends, gave Sheelagh the reason for her depression.

She dreaded Zoe's arrival! It was as simple as that. Yet at the same time, she wanted Zoe to come. But she also wanted Zoe to like her, to gradually learn to love her. Somehow she must make Zoe a good mother or else Luke would feel, even if he didn't admit it, that she had let him down. How did you make a difficult child love you? Especially when you understand how she feels. At least having Mrs Hamilton there would be a help.

The weeks sped by and Sheelagh enjoyed her Christmas with Luke alone. On Boxing Day they went to Moroni and Sheelagh met Mercury's wife, a small frail-looking woman with once-red hair and anxious eyes.

Diane Potter said: 'Mercury thinks the world of you, Sheelagh.'

'I like him,' Sheelagh admitted. 'I didn't at first until I understood his sense of humour.'

'I wish I could,' Diane confessed. 'But I

take everything seriously and that annoys him.'

Mercury had a very luxurious penthouse flat with a superb view. After a delicious meal of seafood, the two men began to talk shop and Diane sighed, lifting her eyebrows significantly to Sheelagh.

'Let's go into the other room,' Diane suggested.

Sitting alone with Mercury's wife in the gorgeously furnished sitting-room, looking out over the lagoon, Sheelagh found herself wondering what had made this nice woman marry him if she found him so frightening.

'Marriage changes men,' Diane said, startling Sheelagh with her bluntness. 'Mercury was so different. Of course, much slimmer, not a tenth as rich, but much more of a husband when we were first wed. All he thinks of now is his work. He began to make jokes that I didn't find funny, and to this day, I never know when he's really mad at me.' She smiled. 'But there you are, eh, Sheelagh? You love a man so you put up with everything. I'm glad Luke has married you.'

'Thank you.' Sheelagh was a little embarrassed, wondering what Diane was going to say next.

Diane was smiling. 'You're young, intelligent, willing to adapt yourself to your new life – the complete opposite to Gina.'

'You knew her?' Tentatively, Sheelagh asked the question, not sure if Luke would mind, for he had so constantly said they were to forget Gina, she was the past!

How they would forget her once her daughter and mother had come out, Sheelagh often wondered, but perhaps Luke would explain to Mrs Hamilton his desire not to dig up past sorrows. If so, that would prove how much he still loved his first wife, Sheelagh was thinking unhappily.

'Very well. She used to come to me in despair. I can't think why, but she had imagined Luke was a very wealthy business tycoon. When she discovered his job was to try to dig the lonely island out of its primitiveness and turn it into a paying holiday resort she was furious. I think she expected a mansion. She loved our house. I hate it.'

'But why? I thought it was beautiful when Mercury showed it to me.'

'That's why I hate it. It's typical of this new Mercury. He has got to show off. He wants people to stare at his mansion and think how wonderful he is. He needs constant praise, recognition. I loathe it. Mercury is a clever man. That's enough for me. I can't think why he has to show off all the time.'

Sheelagh hesitated. 'He's...'

'Like a little boy. I know.' Diane sighed. 'Men are all the same. Just like children, needing their egos boosted – that's why they marry us.'

'Who marries who?' Mercury asked as he came floundering into the room. 'Have you heard Luke has engaged some pretty dolly as schoolteacher for his daughter's education?'

'Is that so? Another new face?' Diane's face brightened.

Luke sat on the couch next to her, explaining, while Mercury sat by Sheelagh's side and beamed.

'I hear you're about to become a mother?' he said.

Sheelagh was startled. Was she? Not to her knowledge, so how could Luke have ... then she saw the twinkling in Mercury's one good eye and she understood.

'Zoe, you mean,' Sheelagh laughed. 'I'm not sure she's going to accept me as a mother.'

'It may take time, you know.' Mercury breathed heavily. 'I had a stepma, you know. Hated her till the day she died.'

'You didn't?' Sheelagh was dismayed. 'Why?'

'Well, I don't really know. Maybe because I resented it when she came and took over, bossing us about, telling us how to behave. Me own Mum had never bothered. Just let us do what we liked.'

'You think that's a good thing?'

He looked shocked. ''Course not, except in the kid's eyes. I'm sure in time Zoe will love you, but don't try to jump your fences 'fore they're built,' he said with a loud guffaw. 'Give her time, Sheelagh lass, give her time.'

The day Mrs Hamilton and Zoe were expected was a grey dismal-looking wet one. Luke had gone to meet them. He had wanted Sheelagh to go with him, but she had used a migraine as an excuse. It was not a lie, as her head ached because she dreaded the arrival of Zoe. Luke said Zoe should see them together, but Sheelagh said she didn't feel like the double sea trip. Finally Luke went alone, spending the night with Mercury and his wife, and as the long, lonely evening passed, Sheelagh began to wish she had gone with him. Even Jackie's company was not enough after Tarantula had left and Sheelagh had sat on the verandah, looking through the rain at the white flecks of surf as the sea came racing in. The frogs were croaking at the top of their voices as if in protest. Sheelagh just sat, not wanting to read or knit or sew. If only she knew of a way to make Zoe like her, she thought anxiously.

There were flowers in the two bedrooms. Everything Sheelagh could think of, she had. But suppose Zoe took one look at her and threw a tantrum? Luke would be furious with her and Zoe would blame Sheelagh for it.

At last she went to bed, but not to sleep. She tossed and turned, trying to imagine herself as Zoe. Going to a strange land, going to meet a stranger who was her father, having a stepmother, someone who was supposed to take the place of her own mother. Not, Sheelagh reminded herself, that Zoe had ever known her real mother, for few, if any, people can remember what happened when they were eighteen months old.

By the time the car came and the tall exhausted-looking Mrs Hamilton arrived with Luke, and Zoe, who looked as if she had grown taller in the few months since Sheelagh had seen her, ran through the heavy rain up the steps.

'What a horrible day!' Sheelagh exclaimed as she went to meet them, helping Mrs

211

Hamilton off with her wet raincoat and taking Zoe's as well.

Zoe looked at her, her face cold. 'I love the rain,' she said.

Luke laughed as he bent to kiss Sheelagh. 'Just as well,' he said cheerfully, 'because this is the wet season.'

Sheelagh took them to their bedrooms and Zoe looked round curiously. 'I thought it would be a big house,' she said.

'The snaps made it look bigger,' Mrs Hamilton explained. She smiled at Sheelagh. 'It's been quite a journey.'

'It was nothing, Gran,' Zoe said scornfully. 'You do fuss so!'

'Would you like a shower or bath? Tarantula is making some tea,' Sheelagh asked.

'Yes, I would like a shower,' said Mrs Hamilton. 'I feel so hot and sticky. The ship was very small, we bounced about.'

'But, Gran,' Zoe chimed in, 'that's the whole fun of it.'

'I'm afraid I don't enjoy it either,' said Sheelagh.

Zoe looked at her, her eyes cold. 'I can imagine,' she said. 'I'm going to talk to my daddy,' she announced, and walked off.

'Oh dear,' Mrs Hamilton sighed. 'I'm

afraid she's in one of her difficult moods.'

Sheelagh smiled. 'Don't worry. I expect it's all rather a big upheaval for her. She'll settle down.'

Wishful thinking if ever there was any, Sheelagh was to think as the days passed, but now while Mrs Hamilton had a shower, she went back to join the others. She paused outside the open door as she heard Luke's voice.

'That's very sweet of you, Zoe, to offer to look after me, but you still have to go to school for many years. Besides, I love Sheelagh. She's my wife, so she must never leave me.'

'Why did Mummy leave you?' Zoe asked. She spoke quietly, not accusingly at all.

'I don't know,' said Luke. He sounded tired. 'Honestly, Zoe, I don't know. I've often wished I did.'

'You didn't want her to? I mean, you didn't throw her out?' Zoe asked, and Sheelagh's eyes were smarting. Yes, she would have wanted to know that had she been Zoe. But whether she could have asked those questions, she didn't know.

'No, I most certainly did not want her to go,' said Luke, and Sheelagh hurried to their bedroom, then locked herself in the bathroom, her hands over her face, for the jealousy she had thought she had overcome had returned in full strength.

Luke had been speaking the truth. She had heard it in his voice. No, he had not wanted Gina to go. He had loved Gina. Never would he forget her.

In the weeks that followed, Sheelagh felt that Gina had come to life and was living with them. Maybe it was largely Mrs Hamilton's unintentional fault, for she was always saying to Sheelagh or to Luke,

'Zoe gets more like Gina every day.'

Luke would smile and nod, not seeming to mind. It was Sheelagh who did mind, though she never showed it! Zoe, too, was always asking Luke questions about her mother and he would answer patiently.

Zoe was a real Jekyll and Hyde, Sheelagh was soon to learn. When Luke was there, Zoe was a quiet well-behaved girl, scrupulously, almost formally, polite to Sheelagh, but the instant he was out of hearing, Zoe was herself, being rude, cheeky and difficult. When Luke was away and they ate meals alone, Zoe would complain about everything. When Luke was there, she would say how she loved this life.

Caroline Bourne, the English schoolteacher, arrived. A pretty, red-haired girl in her mid-twenties, she was still recovering from a bad car accident. Zoe took an immediate liking to her. Every morning, after breakfast, Luke drove Zoe to the school that was several miles away. Sheelagh and Mrs Hamilton would fetch her at three o'clock, and often Caroline came back to spend the rest of the day with them.

Mrs Hamilton, after she had once grown used to the humidity and heavy rain, grew restless as she was not used to having nothing to do, she, without meaning to, Sheelagh felt sure, took over the cooking and running the house. Tarantula didn't seem to mind, though there was difficulty in communications between them because Tarantula's English left much to be desired and Mrs Hamilton's French was even worse.

So Sheelagh suddenly found herself the odd man out. Zoe didn't need her and showed no desire at all to be friendly, especially now she had Caroline. The house didn't need her, for Mrs Hamilton so obviously enjoyed having something to do. Even Luke seemed to have little use for his wife these days as they were never alone except when they went to bed, and usually Luke was too tired or had work he wanted to do while she went to sleep, to have time to talk.

There were times when Sheelagh felt that if she heard the name Gina again, she would scream and scream and scream.

Gina was dead. Let her stay dead and not come back to life to ruin Luke's second marriage. Maybe, Sheelagh thought, she was getting irritable, for several times she had seen Luke look at her, puzzled. He had even once suggested that she show more affection for his daughter.

That had really hurt. How do you show affection to a lump of stone? she felt inclined to say. Zoe, who was so pleasant to her in front of him and so hostile when he wasn't there. Sheelagh knew it was absurd, but she found herself unable to do anything. Zoe was scornful of Sheelagh's paintings. Sheelagh had little belief in her own talent as an artist – despite the sight of the splotched-on painting Luke had had framed and that hung on the bedroom wall – and although she knew it was absolutely ridiculous to allow an eleven-year-old girl's scorn to hurt, yet hurt it did. Sheelagh found her fingers growing lethargic, even clumsy, so her knitting and sewing was left alone. Her only respite was in translating Mercury's manuscripts. So usually when Zoe was at home, Sheelagh would vanish into the part of the verandah Luke had divided off for her little study. There Sheelagh could concentrate on the often difficult translation and only hear in the distance Zoe's laughter, and Caroline's and Mrs Hamilton's voices.

Perhaps the hardest thing was to write letters to her father. Sheelagh knew she must hide from him how intensely unhappy she was, for hers was no longer a marriage. She and Luke were rarely alone.

But what really hurt was the fact that apparently he didn't mind. He didn't miss their lovely long evenings alone, listening to the radio, talking, or even dancing with the lights low. That never happened now. Sometimes when she saw Luke looking at Zoe, Sheelagh wondered how much longer she could bear it – the love on Luke's face, the gentle way he touched Zoe's hair, his smile. Then Sheelagh would mumble an excuse and hurriedly leave the room, making for the sanctuary of the bathroom where she knew she was safely alone, and if she wept, she could always bathe her eyes in cold water.

One afternoon Mrs Hamilton had gone to bed. For some unknown reason her arthritis, which had been very much better since she came to stay with them, had got worse, so she went to lie down, a hot water bottle against her back. Sheelagh had driven through the heavy rain and mud to the school to fetch Zoe, and when the child saw Mrs Hamilton was not there, she stood still.

'I'm not coming home until Daddy fetches me,' she told Sheelagh.

Caroline came out. 'What's the problem?' she asked.

'Are you coming with us?' Sheelagh began, but Caroline shook her head. 'If you don't mind, no, Sheelagh. I simply must catch up with my letters.'

'I want to stay with you,' Zoe announced. 'I don't want to go home.'

'I'm afraid you can't stay,' Caroline said in that kind but firm voice that Zoe always accepted. 'I'm expecting a visitor, too. See you in the morning, Zoe.'

Sheelagh suppressed a sigh of relief as Zoe got in the car by her side, for she had wondered if Zoe would give way to an attack of tantrums.

They drove home in silence, the car skidding on the muddy roads, the rain pounding on the windscreen so hard that the wipers could not move.

'You don't drive as well as Daddy,' Zoe said proudly.

'I know, but he's been driving much longer than I have,' Sheelagh answered, deftly cornering on a bad turn.

'You killed my mother, didn't you?' said Zoe.

'I did ... *what?*' Startled, Sheelagh looked at her companion and the car skidded. Sheelagh was busy for a few moments getting back on the track, for luckily it was flat ground where they were at that moment. 'What made you say that?'

Zoe, her arms folded, her legs crossed as she sat upright, answered promptly, ''Cos it follows. You wanted my daddy and so you killed Mummy.' She said it all so casually as if murdering a woman because you wanted her husband was an everyday happening, Sheelagh thought, so it helped her laugh.

'Of course I didn't. Why, the year your mummy died, I was your age.'

'My age?' Zoe was surprised. 'I wouldn't kill anyone.'

'Neither would I,' said Sheelagh. If only the road wasn't so difficult! It was only necessary for her to skid off the road, into a tree, and Zoe would accuse her of trying to kill Luke's child!

'Why did Mummy leave Daddy?' Zoe asked. Actually it was the first time they had been really alone together, so Sheelagh thought, in a way she should be glad of the chance of getting Zoe to know her. But heavy rain and slushy slippery roads were not the background to an intimate conversation.

'I haven't a clue. I never knew your mother,' she said, rather impatiently.

'Well, I want to know,' Zoe told her. 'I mean to know, too. It must have been someone's fault. I'm sure it wasn't Daddy's fault, though she said it was.'

'Hold tight,' said Sheelagh. 'This is going to be a bounce.' Even as she spoke they came on the deep rain-filled rut, down, then up, bouncing, the mud and water flying up to dirty the windscreen still more. Fortunately she could see the ocean ahead. Just round the corner would be home. 'Phew! What a journey! I hate this weather.'

Zoe looked ahead, arms tightly folded. 'I like it. I always like...'

Everything you hate, Sheelagh finished the sentence silently, wondering if she would ever break down the barrier between herself and Zoe.

It was twenty minutes later, lying in a lukewarm bath, that Sheelagh remembered something Zoe had said. At the time she had just seen that deep rut ahead across the road, but somehow the words had stayed in her mind.

'*I'm sure it wasn't Daddy's fault, though she said it was.*'

Who was *she?* Sheelagh shivered. It could only be one person: Viola Whittaker!

CHAPTER 10

Sheelagh had read in an article once that no newly married couple should have relatives or friends to live with them. At the time, she had thought it nonsense, but now, as the weeks became months, she realised just how true it was. The magical evenings she and Luke had spent were gone for ever. As soon as he came home, Zoe would rush to meet him, clinging to his arm, asking questions about his work, obviously thrilled to see him. This Sheelagh could understand, for she knew how much she loved her own father and how she had always run to meet him when he came home from work.

But as the evening wore on, there would

be Mrs Hamilton knitting or sewing, her eyes a little clouded sometimes as if memories were sad. That would make Sheelagh looked quickly at Luke as she tried to imagine life without him. It left her with a sick emptiness inside her.

Another problem was that no matter how hard she tried to be friends with Zoe, the girl still refused to let her be. The days dragged by, but the evenings were worse, for each time Sheelagh looked at Luke and he was gazing at his child, she felt again the fear that he never had and never would forget Gina, his first wife.

Perhaps what made it even harder to bear was the fact that Sheelagh loved Zoe; understanding the girl's antagonism, her refusal to accept a stepmother. After all, Zoe had only just discovered her own father, naturally she wanted him to herself, so of course she resented Sheelagh's existence. But if the relationship between the three of them was to be a success, Sheelagh knew she must – simply must – find some way to make Zoe like her, but it seemed impossible and everything seemed to get worse for Sheelagh until the final straw came.

She had slipped away to bed early, feeling she could no longer stand Zoe's chatter, the way Luke smiled at her, Mrs Hamilton's quiet voice joining in – a little threesome with Sheelagh on the outskirts, trying in vain to be part of the family. Yet how could she be when they constantly talked of someone she had never known: Gina! Zoe was full of questions about her mother. Had she liked pop music, did she travel, had she many friends. It was as if Zoe was building up an image of the mother she had never known, in this way bringing herself and her father closer together.

Sheelagh was feeling tired and depressed, for Mercury had said to give Zoe time, but it seemed that the 'time' would last for ever. Once in bed, she was startled to hear the door open, as it was still early. Luke came in, frowning. He closed the door behind him and came to sit on her side of the bed, looking at her.

'What's wrong?' he asked curtly.

'Nothing's wrong. What do you mean?' Sheelagh asked.

'You know very well what I mean. Your behaviour. Your cold indifference to Zoe – letting Mrs Hamilton do all the work while you laze around, looking bored to death. You don't even join our talks, you sit there, looking like a stone image.' His voice was angry and impatient. 'I thought we agreed to help Zoe together. You leave everything to me and you're hurting her as well.'

'Hurting her?' Sheelagh sat up in bed, her hair a cloud behind her head, her eyes bright with unshed tears. 'What about how she's hurting me ... how you all are? I'm shut out. You talk about Gina, Gina, Gina all the time. I feel like screaming! You told me Gina was in the past and best forgotten, but now we have Gina in every other sentence. Gina whom I never knew. Neither did Zoe, and it's natural that she wants to know all she can about her mother. Even about who killed her...'

'Killed her? Killed Gina? What the hell are you talking about?'

'You ask Zoe. She accused me of killing her mother so that I could marry you. Then, when I explained that I was about her age when her mother died, she said she didn't think *you* killed her mother though "she" said so. She didn't say a name, she just said *she*. I can guess who *she* was, can't you? Mrs Hamilton hates Viola as I do, but Viola's clever enough to have met the child alone and goodness knows how much poison she has put in Zoe's mind – and that's probably why I can get nowhere with her.'

'Do you try?' he asked sarcastically.

Sheelagh looked away. 'If you only knew just how much I try! Maybe I try too hard. Zoe wants you and no one else. I don't blame her, but...' Anger began to erupt inside her, though she fought to control it. 'As for Mrs Hamilton, she took over organising everything. She was bored to tears and asked if she could help. I felt sorry for her, so I let her, and before I knew what was happening, it was no longer my home but hers. I've felt like an unwanted guest with nothing to do, and certainly no husband.'

'Don't be ridiculous! We agreed that Zoe must be treated gently, given time to adjust. You're just making everything twice as hard. I can't think why you're carrying on like this. It's so unlike you.'

'Me? It's always me that's in the wrong. How do you think I feel having Gina thrust down my throat every ten minutes?' Sheelagh's cheeks were a bright red, she was so angry she could hardly get the words out of her mouth. 'No one thinks of how I feel. I don't matter. I'm just the mistake you made.' Her voice thickened and the tears were so near that she turned away quickly.

At that moment there was a piercing scream, followed by another and another.

Luke stood up. 'What the...? The child must have got hurt!'

Sheelagh turned, the tears rolling down her cheeks. 'Don't worry,' she said bitterly. 'She's just having an attack of tantrums because you're with me. Her grandmother can't stop her, only Caroline can. But then Caroline isn't me. You'll see, the instant you go out, she'll stop screaming and look so innocent and hurt that you'll ... you'll probably ... probably say it was my fault she had the tantrums. Get out, Luke ... get out!' she screamed at him, turning to hide her face in the pillow.

He bent down and put his hands on her shoulder. 'Sheelagh, are you feeling ill? This is so unlike you.'

She turned her face, startled to find it so near his.

'I'm tired of being meek little me, doing everything you want, scared to open my mouth in case I annoy you. I'm tired of Gina. When I wanted to talk about her, you said it was in the past – but now it's here. In the present. Every moment of the day I have to think about Gina! I'm sick to death of...'

'All right, if that's how you feel,' he said coldly, standing above her, then going out of the room. As the door opened, the screams came loudly and then abruptly stopped. Sheelagh nodded as she mopped the tears away. At least Luke would have to admit she was right about that!

Quickly she put out the light and lay very still, her eyes tightly closed. She felt absolutely drained of all energy.

She must be asleep when Luke came to bed. She was not going to use her tears as a weapon, nor did she feel in the mood for another row. Somehow she must go to sleep.

But she couldn't, and her body stiffened when, much later, she heard the door open. Obviously Luke was surprised to find the light was out, for he stood there for a few minutes. She wondered if he'd switch it on, wake her up and start it all over again – would he once again accuse her of it being her fault? She bit her lower lip, trying to keep her breathing steady as if she was asleep.

He moved round the room noiselessly, finally climbing into bed by her side. She lay very still indeed, fighting the longing to put out her hand and touch him. If only she could be sure he would turn and take her in his arms, kissing her until she could hardly breathe, whispering in her ear how much he loved her, how sorry he was, that he hadn't realised it was so difficult for her ... but supposing he didn't? Suppose he pushed her away and said he was tired? Supposing he had stopped loving her, giving the love that had been hers to Zoe, his child?

Soon he was asleep. She could tell by his heavy breathing. She lay very still, wondering if she had done wrong, if she should have turned to him and tried, calmly, to make him see it from her point of view? Had she done their marriage a great harm by not making up the quarrel? What was it her father had always said?

'Never let the sun go down on a quarrel, Sheelagh love. Always say you're sorry – even if you're not. A quarrel that lasts days is far harder to make up than one of a few hours.'

She slept badly, constantly waking and lying very still in case she woke Luke. She knew what she was going to do. Just as the sun rose, she slipped out of bed, quietly moving round the room, collecting and packing some clothes, before having a shower and putting on a light white Dacron dress. In the bathroom, she brushed her hair, twisting it round her head and pinning it up. This was the way Luke hated – a silent symbol of her revolt.

When he awoke, he lifted his eyebrows as he saw the suitcase.

'Going some place?' he asked drily.

'I'm visiting Diane. She's always asking me and I'm not needed here. Mrs Hamilton and Zoe will look after you,' Sheelagh said, her eyes wide as she looked at him.

But he did none of the things she had hoped he would. He didn't grab hold of her, shake her, even hit her. He just shrugged.

'As you please,' he said, and walked into the bathroom.

Sheelagh went through to the dining-room end of the main room. Mrs Hamilton was fussing round happily, correcting Tarantula's laying of the table as she did every day.

'I'm going to stay a few days with Mercury's wife in Moroni. You don't mind?' Sheelagh asked as she took in her suitcase.

Mrs Hamilton smiled. 'Of course not, dear. It's a good idea while I'm here and can look after the family. You need a change, too,' she added shrewdly, a little too shrewdly for Sheelagh's comfort. She didn't want Mrs Hamilton to know the truth – whatever had happened to her marriage was not Mrs Hamilton's fault, she knew. Was it her fault, as Luke would say? Was it due to her terrible jealousy of Gina?

Zoe came dancing in. She saw the suit-case. 'You're going away?' she said to Sheelagh, her face bright with glee, and then it changed as Luke came into the room. 'We'll miss you, won't we, Daddy?' Zoe asked.

'No doubt,' he said curtly.

Breakfast was a difficult meal with Zoe chatting away, Mrs Hamilton unusually silent, her eyes puzzled as she looked from Luke to Sheelagh and then back again.

As they finished, Luke looked down the table at Sheelagh.

'We'll drop Zoe off at school and then I'll drive you to the jetty. Is Diane expecting you?'

'No ... no, she isn't,' said Sheelagh, suddenly confused, conscious of Mrs Hamilton's troubled eyes. 'She said to go as soon as I could. This seems a good chance, as the rain has stopped.'

'It stopped a week ago,' Luke said coldly as he stood up, glancing at his watch. 'Three minutes, Zoe, or you'll have to walk.'

Zoe laughed happily. 'You wouldn't do that to me, Daddy,' she said proudly, and darted out of the room. Luke went in the opposite direction.

Mrs Hamilton hurried to Sheelagh's side. 'My dear, are you sure you're all right? You've eaten no breakfast and I know how you hate the crossing. You're not like yourself.'

'I keep being told that,' said Sheelagh, unable to keep the bitterness out of her voice. 'Sometimes I wonder what the real me is like.'

Mrs Hamilton's eyes were understanding. 'My dear, this is what you learn in marriage,' she said, lowering her voice. 'It's never easy.'

Nor has it been made any easier for us having Zoe and you here, Sheelagh thought desperately. If only Zoe's grandfather had not died...

After they had dropped Zoe off at the thatched-roof school and seen Caroline's friendly face as she waved, one hand lightly on Zoe's shoulder, the drive into the small town was silent. It was only as they reached the jetty and Luke carried her case on board for her, doing the essential formalities, that he spoke, pulling a letter out of his pocket.

'I forgot to give this to you yesterday,' he said bluntly. 'I didn't know you had a friend in America.'

'America?' Sheelagh turned the envelope over and over and frowned, then she nodded. 'Of course. It's from Tony.'

'Tony Rogers?' Luke asked. 'The man you were going to marry? Does he write often?'

She was puzzled by Luke's tone and suddenly excited, for he sounded jealous, and if he was jealous of Tony, then...?

'Not often. He isn't a good letter writer. I wonder how he got my address.' She stuffed the envelope into her handbag, for bells were clanging, shouts piercing the sunny day's beauty as the boat got ready to leave.

'Have a good time,' said Luke, looking down at her, but not attempting to touch her. Her hope that he was jealous vanished instantly.

Shivering a little, Sheelagh tried to smile. 'I will.'

'You'll come back?' he asked casually, almost as if it was of no importance.

'Of course.'

He gave a wry smile. 'Famous last words? I wonder,' he said, and walked off the boat, walking down the jetty without turning once to wave goodbye.

'He said it just as if he didn't care,' Sheelagh sobbed as she sat in Diane Potter's luxurious flat telling her about it all. 'As if he didn't care. He didn't even turn to wave to me.'

'He was probably afraid you'd see how upset he was,' the older woman said gently.

Sheelagh looked up, startled. 'You think so?'

'I don't think, I know.' Diane spoke with

unusual firmness. 'I've known Luke for a long time and I'll never forget the state he was in when Gina walked out. It would be even worse now, because he loves you.'

'But does he? I want to think he does, but surely he can see how ... how awful it is for me?'

'I doubt it very much. Have you thought that it's pretty awful for him?' Diane asked as the slender island girl brought in a tray of food for Sheelagh. 'Now eat that up like a good girl,' Diane said, firm again. 'We can't have you getting ill.'

Sheelagh obeyed, sitting at the table, eating slowly as Diane talked thoughtfully.

'Try to imagine it from Luke's point of view.' Diane lifted a hand. 'No, don't protest. I'm on your side, too, but let's look at it from Luke's first. He's never been sure why Gina left him. He's never said much, but I could tell from what he did that he always thought it was his fault, that he had expected too much of Gina, that he had treated her badly.'

'But...'

'Exactly. I'm sure Luke didn't treat Gina any worse than any young man, ambitious, working hard with thought of the future before him, could do. Life is not a bed of roses, and any girl with sense when she

marries knows this. Marriage is a partner-
ship – she can't expect everything to be
perfect for her. Unfortunately Gina did. She
had a grudge against the world because she
was not born a wealthy princess.' Diane
laughed and Sheelagh joined in.

'Anyhow, Luke felt he was at fault, that he
was a bad husband. Now he marries again.
After considerable thought, I understand.'

Sheelagh's tears had dried, now she could
nod with a smile. 'He told me he deliberately stayed away from me for two months
in an attempt to forget me.'

'I can believe that. Typical of your husband. Luke's no fool. He'd made a mistake
once, he didn't want to make it again. So he
married you. Gina was in the past, best
forgotten. Your marriage was blossoming
beautifully. You had shown what a sensible
girl you were, you adapted yourself. Mercury tells me a lot about you. Then ... then
this happens and the past is dug up again
and there's nothing he can do about it. Is
there?' Diane looked at Sheelagh, who was
silent. 'Is there?' Diane insisted.

'Well, no, I suppose not.'

'Of course there isn't, Sheelagh. I expect
he hates this constant talk of Gina as much
as you. Like twisting the dagger in a wound.'

She smiled. 'Maybe I'm being a bit dramatic. Anyhow, Luke's first thought is for Zoe. You told him that. Didn't you?' Another silence as Sheelagh stared at Diane. 'Didn't you?' Again Diane insisted.

Sheelagh nodded. 'Yes, I did. I didn't realise.'

'Exactly. The point is this – Luke thought you were both going to cope with this problem. He thought you were mature enough to realise he has long forgotten Gina, apart from a sense of guilt about her which is, of course, typical of Luke – that you would understand he had to put up with Zoe's constant questions and Mrs Hamilton's natural talk of her only child. This was to be expected. Do you honestly think it's any easier for Luke than it is for you?'

'I never thought of it like that.' Sheelagh went back to curl up on the couch as the maid brought in coffee for both. 'I was so jealous, so terribly jealous of Gina that ... that...' She bit her lip.

Diane smiled. 'I would have felt the same. Don't worry, you're not being any different from other girls. Of course we're jealous of our husband's first loves. It was even worse for you learning about it as you did. Luke should have told you beforehand. Yet I can

235

understand that, too, though I don't expect you to, Sheelagh. Luke met you – the perfect girl, the one he really loved. Gina was in the past, and he had forgotten her. Then that terrible woman...'

Her hands round her knees on which her chin rested, Sheelagh told Diane how Zoe kept asking why and how her mother died, and how it happened.

'We were in the car,' Sheelagh began, then told Diane everything, finishing by saying: 'Actually it was some time later that I remembered Zoe had said "I don't believe Daddy killed her, though *she* said so." I wondered who *she* could be. I knew it wasn't Mrs Hamilton, for she has always been on Luke's side, and then I thought of Viola Whittaker. I'm sure that's why Zoe hates me so much.'

'Sheelagh dear,' Diane's voice was gentle, 'it would have been a miracle if Zoe loved you already. Don't feel you've failed Luke. You haven't. You've done your best. Only time can make Zoe accept you as her father's wife. She may never be able to see you as a mother, or even a stepmother.'

'I know, but...'

'But me no buts,' Diane teased. 'I'm glad you came to me, but why did you?'

Sheelagh hesitated. 'Luke told me you love Mercury so much even though ... even though you can't understand his funny sense of humour, so I thought ... well, I love Luke and ... and I'm frightened. I think he...'

'He loves you, Sheelagh, have no fear of that. Your marriage is going through a difficult phase. But it will go through many more and perhaps even worse phases. Marriage means learning how to get through these phases *together* – not fighting one another at the same time. It won't be easy, but go home and put up with Gina, even ask questions yourself. Let Luke see that you're letting Mrs Hamilton take over to make her happy, not yourself. Praise her cooking, but go to your easel and paint.'

'Zoe thinks it's awful.' Sheelagh blushed. 'I know it's stupid of me to mind what a kid of eleven says, but...'

'You're in a sensitive, tense state, Sheelagh. She's probably being loyal to her mother, who couldn't paint, so she doesn't want Daddy to know that you can do something her own mother couldn't do.'

'I never thought of that. It makes sense,' Sheelagh said slowly. 'Diane, you are wonderful. How do you know so much?'

Diane laughed. 'I'm a great deal older

than you, Sheelagh, and have been married for over forty years. That teaches you!'

'I felt frightfully guilty about feeling jealous. Dad says it's the worst disease in the world.'

'We all feel guilty about something or other,' Diane said with a smile. 'I feel guilty because I won't live in Mercury's marvellous house. At the same time, I know he doesn't really like it, not as he likes here where we're more in the middle of things. Did Luke tell you Mercury and I are off to South America next month? Mercury has some new bright idea and must investigate it first himself. As for jealousy, some people are lucky enough to have sufficient self-confidence and trust in each other, but not all of us have.'

'I tried to make Luke jealous,' said Sheelagh. 'That reminds me,' she went on, jumping up to get her handbag.

'If he was, he wouldn't show it,' Diane said as Sheelagh took out the letter Luke had given her.

'This letter's from Tony Rogers,' Sheelagh said, briefly telling Diane about the engagement that had been a mistake. 'We were always good friends and I'm fond of him, but marriage? Definitely no. I wonder why he's written to me. It's years since...'

'Well, open it and see,' Diane told her with a smile. 'I've a phone call to make.'

Left alone, Sheelagh opened the envelope. There were two letters inside. Why on earth had Tony bothered to write? They'd drifted so far apart.

She read the letters, her face wrinkling up in amazement, and looked up just as Diane returned.

'You should just hear this,' Sheelagh said.

'Okay, read it to me,' Diane told her, sitting on the couch with her natural grace. 'I've left my glasses somewhere, so I can't see.'

'All right. I just can't believe it! It could only be...' Sheelagh muttered, staring at the two letters in her hand.

'You're not reading,' Diane said gently.

'Sorry, I'll read Tony's first.' Sheelagh took a deep breath. 'Dear Sheelagh, I was terribly upset and shocked to hear what a disaster your marriage has turned out to be, especially as I am happily married myself. I would have thought you'd make a perfect wife, but it seems it's your husband's fault, as he ruined his first marriage through his selfishness and brutality. The letter also said that you would never tell your parents as it

239

would upset them too much. It so happened that my wife and I are about to visit England to meet my people, so I'm planning to fly out quickly to the island to see if I can give you some advice and help.' Sheelagh looked up from what she was reading. 'He's a lawyer, you see.'

'I see, go on.'

'Where was I? Oh yes, so I can give you some advice and help. We grew up together and although you were so right in saying we should not marry, I shall always be fond of you and can't bear to think of you as being not only unhappy but perhaps in danger. I've booked everything and shall be arriving in Moroni Airport on the fifteenth.' Sheelagh looked up. 'That's tomorrow!' She went back to the letter. 'I'm afraid I can only stay for a night as we have so much to see in so short a time, but I shan't be happy unless I can help you out of the mess you've found yourself in. You will see from the enclosed letter why I'm so worried about you.'

Sheelagh put the letter down and picked up the other. 'Of course you've guessed what it is, Diane,' she said. 'It's from that awful woman again.'

'Viola?' Diane asked. 'But how would she know about him? I mean, she didn't know your family.'

'*Didn't* is right, but I forgot to tell you that some way back Dad in a letter told me a friend of Luke's who had been to the wedding called to visit them. Then when I went back to England to arrange about Zoe I stayed a couple of nights with my parents. Dad said he had little to do with Viola, but I remember now that Mum looked rather upset and said she wished I'd warned her. Now I can see it, Viola must have got Mum to tell her about Tony to whom I was once engaged, and then, no doubt, she wrote to him and the letter was forwarded to America.'

'What does she say?'

Sheelagh unfolded the other letter, looking at the long spidery writing. 'You can imagine! Dear Mr Rogers, I am writing to you because I am so anxious about Sheelagh Tysack, who is now Sheelagh Jessop. I know you two were very good friends, indeed nearly married, and there is no one else I can turn to for help. I know Sheelagh will never tell her parents about it in case it worries them, but she is in great trouble. The man she has married, Luke Jessop, has been married before. His wife died – it was all very hush-hush, but it was entirely due to his brutality and indifference. He also has a child whom he deserted and left to the grandparents to bring up. Sheelagh is living on a remote, primitive island, with no friends. Her husband is a bully and I am afraid for her future. Please help her. I can think of no one else who could.' Sheelagh looked up. 'Signed Viola Whittaker. Diane, I ask you! What will she do next? What was her idea anyhow?'

'Perhaps she wanted him to come out and make Luke jealous. Did she know Tony was married?'

'No. Because I didn't know until I went back last time – I mean when I went to arrange about Zoe, Dad told me, but I completely forgot it because...'

'It was of the past,' Diane said with a smile. 'Sensible girl!'

'Tony's coming tomorrow ... all that money spent! He can afford it, though, but how mad his wife must feel about me.'

'A vicious circle,' Diane said with a laugh.

'But why should Viola be so ... so ... well, the absolute end?' Sheelagh asked angrily. 'I'm sure she's been at Zoe, too. Why does she keep implying that Gina was killed?'

'Perhaps she was,' said Diane. Sheelagh looked startled and Diane smiled. 'I don't mean murdered but killed by Viola's maliciousness. Have you ever asked Mrs Hamilton why Gina died?'

'No. I was going to, but ... well, her husband has died quite recently and I didn't like to.'

'You were quite right. Look, I must make another phone call. What do you think we'd better do about your ex-boy-friend?'

'I'll have to meet him tomorrow.' Sheelagh looked at the letters in her hand with a frown. Then she looked up. 'I know – I'll take him back to the Isle of Maloudia with me and he can meet Luke, then he'll realise what a pack of lies the letter was, also Luke will see just how dangerous Viola is. Somehow or other we must find out why Zoe's mother died, otherwise Zoe will never be happy. She simply has to know.'

'I couldn't agree more,' Diane said. 'May I come with you to the airport and Maloudia?'

'Of course. It would be a great help and Mercury would be thrilled.'

Diane smiled. 'Your friend can stay with us in Mercury's house – that will show Tony the kind of friends you have.'

'I think it's a super idea.' Sheelagh sat up, her pale face flushed, the tears vanished. 'What a help you've been, Diane. I never saw anything the right way before.'

'I didn't, either, at your age,' Diane said. 'I nearly lost Mercury by my foolishness and it taught me to look at both sides, to try to understand how he would feel.' She laughed. 'Of course it doesn't always work because so often we women have a totally different outlook from men, bless them.' She smiled. 'I have enjoyed this talk, Sheelagh. I think it's opened my eyes to something, too,' she added.

'You're thinking of Mercury?'

Diane nodded. 'Yes, what do you think of him? Be honest, now.'

Sheelagh looked round the expensive and tastefully furnished room with its deep comfortable armchairs, the shining silver, sparkling glass. Everything a man could give his wife was here – except love. Yet men felt that was what a wife wanted. Money. Of course some did – like Gina.

'All right,' Sheelagh said, feeling the long talk with Diane had amazingly lessened the age gap between them and had given her a friend she could talk frankly to. 'When I first met Mercury, I was terrified.' She smiled ruefully at Diane, who nodded understandingly. 'He seemed sarcastic, antagonistic, everything. He mocked at brides and marriages and accused me of marrying Luke for

244

his money. I lost my temper and shouted at him. I was rather upset, but ... but Mercury loved it. He said he liked someone to fight back at him, and ... and...' Sheelagh wasn't sure whether to repeat all Mercury had said would be wise. 'Anyhow, he said he liked people to fight back. I think ... I think he'd like you to,' she added, and then wondered if it was wise.

Diane Potter was certainly not annoyed. Her eyes were twinkling.

'You think he'd like it if I fought back? Instead of keeping my mouth shut?'

'He told me he married you because you were a beautiful redhead and that redheads have bad tempers, so he looked forward to fights.'

'And I never fought?'

'No.' Sheelagh paused, because Diane had begun to laugh and kept on laughing until the tears ran down her cheeks.

'Bless you, Sheelagh, for telling me that,' Diane said, looking at her watch. 'Let's bath and dress up and we'll go out to dinner to the new restaurant. Mercury is away, but he says it should be a hit with the tourists ... by the way, Sheelagh, we didn't finish what you were saying. You were afraid of him at first?'

'Yes. Then he did some very thoughtful

things to help me get settled here and ... and I grew to like him. Now I like him very much.'

Diane smiled. 'I'm glad. So do I.'

Each bedroom had its own bathroom and as Sheelagh soaked in the warm water, she thought of Tony and the letter. How typical of Tony to drop everything and come to her rescue. All those years they had grown up together, he had protected her. Maybe that was why she had slid into the engagement, that and their parents' approval, perhaps. She wondered who he had married. It sounded like an American girl, if he had taken her over to England to meet his parents. What would Luke say when he saw Viola's letter? Surely there must be something they could do to stop this?

And then thinking of Luke made her remember all that Diane had said. Why, Sheelagh thought, had she never realised it might be just as hard for Luke to have to listen to the constant talk about Gina as it was for her? Why hadn't she had sense enough to know this and to have accepted it? Why hadn't she faced the truth – that it was impossible to hope that Zoe could love her for a long time.

If only she would, Sheelagh thought sadly.

Zoe was a nice girl, for all her tantrums to get attention, for her blunt questions. No one could blame Zoe for wanting to know how or why her mother had died. Sheelagh knew that in Zoe's place, she would have asked the same questions.

They watched the plane come down with its graceful efficiency at Moroni Airport and saw the passengers slowly get out, go into the small bus that took them to collect their luggage.

'What is Tony like?' Diane asked as they waited. 'Is he like Luke?'

'Not in the least,' Sheelagh told her, turning to smile. 'He's as tall as Luke, but very thin. He's got longish dark hair and dark eyes. He's a darling, rather pompous at times and with real old-world manners.'

'You nearly married him?'

'Yes, I drifted into it. I felt safe with him, at ease. So very different from how I felt with Luke. Luke was the most exciting person I'd ever met.'

At last the tall, dark-haired man came hurrying towards them.

'Sheelagh!' he exclaimed, holding out his hands. He looked puzzled. 'You don't look ill.'

'Oh, Tony, it's lovely to see you, but the whole thing was a mistake. Look, we have to catch a boat, so we mustn't talk now. This is Diane Potter, her husband is Luke's partner. Diane ... oh, I'm saying it the wrong way round as usual,' she laughed.

Tony laughed, too, and shook Diane's hand, his eyes puzzled. 'I'm sure I've seen you somewhere. Were you in the States last year?'

Diane smiled. 'Yes, my husband and I were.'

Tony clicked his fingers. 'I've got it! Your husband's known as Mercury. Am I right?'

'Quite right,' Diane told him. 'I think we should hurry, Sheelagh, the plane is late and we must catch the ship. It only goes once a day each way,' she explained to Tony.

He looked round. 'You know, this is quite a place. I've brought practically nothing with me as I must go back soon.'

The car was waiting for them and the big-smile driver, and soon they were speeding along. 'Have a look at everything, Tony,' Sheelagh said. 'I'll explain about the letter on the ship. Look at that lovely mosque ... and here's the market place. Did you see those gorgeous orchids? We grow masses of them and a lovely flower called ylang-ylang.

I'd never heard of it, but it grows here and they send it to French perfume houses...' She talked excitedly, her face happy. 'The trouble is when you live in a beautiful place, you're apt to take it for granted and just don't see it any more.'

'How right you are,' Diane Potter agreed.

The ship was ready to leave, but they got on it in time. Diane knew the captain and went to lie on the couch in his cabin.

'I'm not a good sailor,' she confessed.

Sheelagh and Tony walked along the decks, Sheelagh holding his arm when the ship rolled, feeling as if the years had fallen away and she was young Sheelagh who had adored her next-door neighbour.

'Tony, I'm sorry you've been brought out here for nothing,' she began. 'But it's good to see you.'

'You certainly don't look ill or as if you had a bully for a husband. What's it all about?'

As they walked, stopping now and then to lean on the rail and watch the huge waves that came to toss them in the air, Sheelagh told him the whole story: from Viola Whittaker's words in the church chancel right up to the letter she had sent to him. 'Viola and Luke's first wife were more than good friends, Gina was her adoring shadow, both her mother and Luke say, then when Gina married Luke, Viola seemed to have sworn revenge. I don't know why – she was years older than Luke.'

'Age has nothing to do with such matters,' Tony announced in his rather pedantic fashion. 'Often an older woman can be more maliciously jealous than a young one. What's her idea? To wreck any marriage your husband has?'

'That's what I think, and then there's Zoe,' Sheelagh sighed, telling him how antagonistic Zoe was. 'Not that I blame her. If you've just found the father you've always wanted, then I'm sure it's natural to hate your stepmother. All the same, when she accused me of killing her mother, she said: "I don't believe Daddy did it, though *she* said so." *She* ... there can only be one *she*.'

'What about Gina's mother?'

'She's staying with us, too. She's on Luke's side. She'd never suggest he killed Gina.'

'Whoever this Viola is she's a fool,' Tony said, as they leant over the rail, splashed by the waves' spray. 'She signs her name and makes no attempt to hide. She could be quite dangerous.'

'That's what I think. After all, it was the meanest thing to do, to write and worry you.'

'I think the meanest thing she did was to tell you at your wedding that Luke had been married before. I can't understand why he hadn't told you, though.'

'I think he wanted to forget the whole thing, it was sort of pushed into the background and never talked about. I mean, there was nothing to hide. Diane ... she's sweet, isn't she?' Sheelagh asked, looking towards the captain's cabin, 'she said Luke has always wondered if it was his fault the marriage was a failure. Diane says definitely not, that Gina expected too much.'

'Poor Sheelagh,' Tony smiled sympathetically. 'You have had a difficult time. Now where do I come into it?'

'Now you're here, I want your help. Luke is so kind he'll let Viola go on doing this for ever. I want it stopped,' Sheelagh told him. 'I'm afraid of the damage she could do to Zoe. That's why I want you to show Luke the letter you received and make him see we *must* do something. I don't know what, but something.' A note of desperation was in her voice. 'Already she nearly ruined our marriage, now I think she's been making Zoe hate me, and now this. It can't go on.'

'I agree,' Tony said quietly, his eyes perturbed as he looked at her. 'But don't you think you're letting it all get out of proportion? A foolish, jealous, malicious woman is trying to hurt you, and you're letting her succeed?'

'I can't help it.' Sheelagh's voice broke. 'You know how easy it is to ... to harm a marriage, Tony, when you're young and ... and don't see things the right way. Diane has been a terrible help. I had no idea I'd been so unutterably stupid. Look, let's forget me and talk about you. How long have you been married, and why didn't anyone know until it was all over?'

They began to walk again, Sheelagh rolling against him as the ship did, and they talked and laughed as Tony described his visit to the States, how he met the girl, the daughter of a well-known politician. 'She didn't want publicity, nor did I, so we just went off quietly. Her parents were furious, so were mine, but I think both are accepting it now.'

Sheelagh laughed. 'It sounds so unlike you. You were always so ... so...'

'Like a sheep, doing what I was told?' Tony laughed. 'I've grown up, Sheelagh, and so have you. How right you were about us marrying. It would never have worked. You are happy? I am. We fight like mad, but it's worth it when we make it up.'

Sheelagh smiled. 'Yes, I am happy, Tony, very happy indeed,' she said. Which would not have been true had he asked her the day before, but was true since Diane had made her see Luke's side of it. 'Look!' she said eagerly. 'There's our island.'

They watched the blur become easy to see, the two tall sky-searching peaks that dominated the huddled small town. Sheelagh told Tony of what Luke and Mercury were doing, how hard he worked, of their plans.

'If he's a partner to Mercury Potter, he's on the right road,' Tony said.

'They've been friends for years. Have you met Mercury? You will. You'll be their guest tonight, but you're all coming to have dinner with us. I think it's time we dug out the whole horrible business and talked about it,' Sheelagh said earnestly. 'We owe it to Zoe. I don't want that child to grow up with a complex about it, thinking we're hiding something from her.'

'I think you're right there,' Tony agreed. 'You love that child?'

'Yes, but I'm afraid she doesn't love me. Give her time, they all say, but...'

'We're expecting a baby,' Tony told her. 'Three months' time.'

'You are?' Sheelagh looked pleased. 'How absolutely gorgeous! You must be thrilled.'

'We are. At the moment, we discuss names for hours on end and so far can't agree.' He laughed. 'When are you starting your family?'

Sheelagh shrugged and then smiled. 'Any day now, I hope. I'm only worried about Zoe. It might make her even more jealous,' she was saying when Diane Potter joined them.

'Nearly over,' she said, looking rather pale. 'You look fine, Sheelagh.'

'We talked so much I forgot about feeling ill,' Sheelagh laughed.

They came close towards the jetty and there, standing in front of the crowd, stood one who could never be overlooked – Mercury himself.

But not Luke, Sheelagh thought, and then reminded herself that Luke had no idea when she was coming back. Obviously Diane had phoned Mercury, but perhaps he had not seen Luke?

'Hullo, hullo, hullo,' grinned Mercury, looking at his wife with dramatic horror. 'For why this great honour, my dear?' he asked, kissing her cheek.

'I thought it was time I checked up on

your behaviour,' Diane smiled, lifting her chin, her frail-looking face bright with amusement.

'You did, now?' Mercury's one good eye twinkled. 'You've left it a bit late, love, but better late than never. It's a real pleasure.' He turned to Sheelagh. 'I know someone who'll be glad to see you back. Want me to tell him?'

Sheelagh hesitated. If Luke came home early? ... but if he didn't? 'Please – but tell him there's no hurry. You're all coming to dinner tonight.'

'Are we? That'll be a pleasure, too,' Mercury chuckled as he turned to Tony and held out his hand. 'Glad to meet you, son. Understand you just escaped the terrible mischance of marrying this young lady.'

Tony smiled. 'We were lucky, though I didn't think so at the time.'

Mercury turned to his wife. 'What's the plan, my darling?'

'I'm taking Tony to our house where he's staying the night and Pierre will take Sheelagh home. We're all expected to dinner. Are you coming with us now?'

'Afraid not. I just felt I should come and welcome my wandering wife home. It's a long time since you spent a night here.'

Diane smiled. 'Too long,' she said.

Mercury escorted them to the car, Tony looking round, Sheelagh explaining eagerly the different buildings, showing him as they drove the lovely sweet-smelling flowers, the hotel, which impressed him, the beauty of the scene, the lovely white sand.

'You really like this place?' Tony asked, a little puzzled as if wondering how anyone could settle down in such a lonely island.

'I love it,' said Sheelagh, which was the truth, but she also knew that if Luke announced that they were going to live in Alaska or at the South Pole, she could be just as happy there. It wasn't the place but the person you were with that counted.

Tony looked rather startled when he saw the mansion on the plateau overlooking the road. Diane was right, Sheelagh thought, it did look out of place in this quiet country-side.

'See you later,' Sheelagh said.

'Yes, we've nice time for a bath and a drink and then we'll be over,' Diane promised.

Sheelagh was driven home, her thoughts busy as she tried to plan how to greet Luke. Vaguely she noticed that they must have had some heavy, unexpected rain. They had parted in such coldness – how could she jump the gap and make it their usual greeting? Yet somehow she must.

Mrs Hamilton was alone. She came to greet Sheelagh eagerly. 'My dear, I am glad you're back. I've been quite worried about you. What did the doctor say?'

'The doctor?' Sheelagh repeated as she went up the steps with Mrs Hamilton. 'But I didn't go to see the doctor.'

'You didn't? Oh dear!' Mrs Hamilton sighed. 'I thought ... I hoped you were pregnant.'

'Me?' Sheelagh began to laugh, and stopped. 'I'm sure I'm not. At least I think I'm not. I am pretty irregular, but...'

'Then you didn't go to see a doctor?'

'No, I went ... well, as I said, I wanted to talk to Diane, Mercury's wife. What made you think I was going to have a baby?'

They both sat down, Tarantula hurrying and puffing as she greeted the Madame and took the suitcase away, bringing back long ice-cold drinks.

'Your whole behaviour. I said so to Luke. He came back for lunch yesterday. You've changed so, Sheelagh, as if you've retreated in a ... well, sort of shell. Don't you want a child?'

'Of course I do, very much indeed. I'm

only worried about Zoe. Wouldn't she be jealous?' Sheelagh sipped the cold drink, welcoming the cool liquid sliding down her hot throat.

'Most certainly not.' Mrs Hamilton leaned forward, her face earnest. 'It's what Zoe needs, to be part of a family, the larger the better. She'd be so proud of a baby brother she could boast about at school. It used to upset her so – all her friends had fathers, mothers, uncles, aunts, brothers, sisters, cousins galore. She had no one, only us, two oldies. She hated Speech Day and Sports Day when the other parents came and she had no one.'

'But didn't Luke go sometimes?'

'Oh yes, but we had decided it was better for her not to know him, either as an uncle or a father, as he could so seldom come. But a baby brother, and perhaps a sister ... that would be wonderful.'

'I don't know how many I can promise,' Sheelagh joked. They both laughed. 'If you don't mind, I'd like a quick shower. We've three visitors for dinner. Have you told Tarantula about dinner?'

'Actually, no. You see, I was a little puzzled. Luke didn't come back last night.'

'Not at all?'

'No, not at all, and I'd arranged a big dinner, so there's quite a lot left over for tonight.'

'It'll keep. I'd better go and see Tarantula, as there'll be seven of us.' As Sheelagh turned away, she saw a brief cloud pass over Mrs Hamilton's face and she remembered something Diane had said, so she turned. 'Mrs Hamilton, would you make us one of your delicious soufflés?'

Mrs Hamilton beamed. 'Of course I will.'

'Would you teach me how to cook some time? You're so good at it,' Sheelagh said.

'Gladly.'

'Where's Jackie?'

'Mrs Nucket borrowed him as her husband was going away. I hope you don't mind?'

'Of course not. Where's Zoe? She must have been upset last night when her father didn't come back?' She waited, hand on the back of the chair, as she looked at Mrs Hamilton.

'Not really, Sheelagh. I thought she might feel lonely, but Luke had planned it all. He lent Caroline a car and she drove Zoe home from school and spent the evening with us. You know, Sheelagh, Zoe is getting so like her mother that in a way it worries me, though I like Caroline very much and she's quite different from that horrible Viola Whittaker. Zoe has what we used to call a schoolgirl crush on Caroline. Zoe, like her mother, needs someone to adore.'

Sheelagh wished it was her whom Zoe adored, but knew it was too much to hope for.

'I'm glad she was all right. I'll be quick,' she added as she turned away.

She was quick. She paid a visit to the kitchen where Tarantula sat knitting and listening to the radio. They examined the contents of the deep freeze and discussed the meal, Tarantula looking pleased as Punch because she loved them to entertain.

Then Sheelagh had a quick shower, her mind as usual chasing itself round. Why hadn't Luke come home to dinner and to sleep the night before? What had he thought when Mrs Hamilton suggested his wife was going to have a baby? she wondered.

Zoe was still not home when Sheelagh rejoined Mrs Hamilton. Tarantula came with the tray of drinks and a big smile at Sheelagh.

'Zoe still not back?' she asked Mrs Hamilton, smoothing down her white crêpe frock, having brushed her hair in the style Luke preferred so that it was like a cloud on her shoulders.

'She's with Caroline, but she'll be back for dinner.' Mrs Hamilton looked a little uncomfortable and Sheelagh wondered why. 'Actually, Sheelagh, I'm glad to have this chance of a talk with you before she comes back. Sheelagh, you've been very sweet and most patient these last months and I want you to know how much I appreciate it. I shall miss you all.'

'But you're not going yet?' Sheelagh was startled.

Mrs Hamilton put up her hand to touch her hair. 'I'm afraid I must, dear. You know the friends who rented my house? Well, one is very ill and in hospital in London, so his wife has gone up there, and I don't like my house standing empty. Also Caroline has a brother who specialises in converting houses into blocks of flats and she suggested I did just that. I'd get the rents and have my own little flat without living on my own.' She lifted her hand. 'Don't forget, Sheelagh, I lived there all my married life and have so many friends there. I think it would work out well.'

'It certainly sounds an excellent idea, because it's a very big house and you have a lovely garden.'

'Yes, and with Zoe at boarding school in Guildford, it wouldn't be too far for me to go down at weekends or have her home for half term. Then she can fly out here for the big holidays.'

'Zoe? Going to boarding school?' Sheelagh could not keep the dismay out of her voice. If that happened, she would never win Zoe's love, for she would blame her father's new wife for it and never forgive her.

But Mrs Hamilton was laughing. 'I was rather surprised, too, Sheelagh, remembering the terrible scene there was when we suggested it in England. It's Caroline's doing. We talked it out last night. Caroline told us that when she came out, she couldn't make up her mind whether or not to marry her boyfriend. He is headmaster of a girls' boarding school. It happens quite often now. I have an idea it began at Roedean,' Mrs Hamilton said with a smile. 'Anyhow, Caroline had a bad shock in the car crash and asked for time to make up her mind. Now she has, and when she goes back, she'll marry him, and Zoe wants to be a pupil at the school.'

'I can't believe it!' Sheelagh was filled with disappointment. She had tried so hard to make friends with Zoe and now the chance was gone for ever. 'I don't know what Luke will say.'

'He thinks it's a fine idea.'

'But I thought he didn't come back last night?' Sheelagh refilled the glasses and went back to her chair.

'He didn't, so I phoned him this morning. I didn't want you both to come home tonight and hear all these plans without warning. I hope you're not hurt, Sheelagh? I mean, you've been so good to both Zoe and me, and...'

Sheelagh managed to smile. 'No, I'm not hurt. I only want her to be happy,' she said, but she knew it was not true, she had wanted Zoe to be happy because of her stepmother! So again, Sheelagh thought miserably, her streak of jealousy had shown. 'Whose idea was it?'

'Actually, Luke's – though I didn't know it. He feels, and I agree with him, that Zoe should be brought up in a wider world than this. Also as Luke said, he doesn't know how long you'll both be living here. With Mercury, he said, you never can tell what bright new idea he'll think up. Luke talked it over with Caroline, it appears, and when she told him about her fiancé, it seemed the answer.

Caroline is a sweet girl and she'll keep in touch with us all.'

'Mrs Hamilton,' Sheelagh began slowly, trying to find the right words, 'I hate discussing this with you as I'm afraid it might hurt, but I do think Zoe should be told how her mother...'

There was the sound of a car drawing up. Mrs Hamilton looked out. 'Perhaps it's Zoe.'

But it wasn't. It was Tony, looking fresh and smart in his dark suit.

He was introduced to Mrs Hamilton and Sheelagh looked down at the car. 'Where are Mercury and Diane?'

Tony looked at her, his eyes narrowed. 'They send their apologies, but Mercury had a previous engagement he can't break and Diane decided to go with him.'

'Did they have a row?' Sheelagh asked as she pointed to a chair and then poured Tony his favourite drink which she remembered.

Tony looked surprised. 'Actually they did. I even heard something hit the door. But Mercury looked in a very good mood and his wife was smiling.'

'Good,' said Sheelagh, and saw the surprise on Mrs Hamilton's face. 'I told Diane that Mercury hated people who don't fight

264

back, so she said she'd try it. It seems to have worked.'

Another car drew up and Zoe came running up the steps.

'Wouldn't Caroline like to stay?' Sheelagh suggested, but Zoe stood in the doorway.

'She's gone. She said she had to write to Uncle Ken and tell him I'm going to be a pupil. Who's that?' she asked Sheelagh, staring at Tony.

'Mr Rogers,' Sheelagh said, 'and this is Zoe.'

Zoe shook hands with an unusual politeness. 'Are you from England? I'm going back soon.'

'I'm visiting England but was born there. However, I live in the States.'

'Why?' Zoe was in one of her questioning moods, Sheelagh saw, so she slipped out to the kitchen to tell Tarantula there would be two less for dinner. She also looked at the time worriedly. Luke was late.

Suppose, she thought – just suppose he didn't come home that night?

They were all sitting on the verandah when Luke came back. Sheelagh was so relieved that she acted impulsively, jumping up, running down the steps to greet him.

'You're so late,' she said.

'You're back soon. I hear we've got visitors.'

'Only one. Luke, I've got so much to tell you.'

'It'll have to wait. I just want to know one thing. Why didn't you tell me you were going to have a baby?'

They were standing in the light from the verandah and Sheelagh knew that at any moment Zoe might run down to join them.

'Because I'm not. At least I don't think I am,' she said.

He frowned. 'Then why did you go to Moroni? Or was it to meet your ex-boyfriend?' His voice was cold and she wondered if she could ever overcome the distance they had grown apart.

'I didn't know he was coming till you gave me that letter. He'd had one from...'

Zoe came down the steps excitedly. 'Daddy, Daddy, we've got a visitor! He lives in America and he's been telling me...'

'Hullo, love.' Luke's voice had the tenderness Sheelagh had noticed was absent when he spoke to her. 'Let's go up and you can introduce me to him.'

Which was what Zoe did, leading her father by the hand, while Sheelagh, her shoulders sagging a little in disappointment, followed them.

Luke shook hands with Tony. 'This is indeed a surprise,' he said.

'It was a greater one for me,' Tony told him. 'Has Sheelagh told you about the letter I got?'

Tarantula's noisy bell clanged the announcement that dinner was ready, so Luke led the way to the dining-room part. As usual the table was beautifully laid, Tarantula puffing and blowing as she moved around, but the food was good and delicious, especially the soufflé.

Zoe did most of the talking, her voice high and eager as she asked Tony questions which he didn't seem to mind answering. Luke was quiet, his face had that retreating look it sometimes had. Sheelagh was almost as quiet, occasionally talking to Mrs Hamilton, who was looking a little anxious as if conscious of the tension.

'What did he mean about the letter he received?' she asked Sheelagh quietly.

'It was from Viola Whittaker,' Sheelagh replied, equally quiet. 'We'll talk about it after dinner.'

Certainly it was more pleasant when they went out on the screen-protected verandah, with the chairs and cushions in a circle round the tray of coffee.

Tony, who was now on friendly terms with Zoe, took the lead, rather to Sheelagh's surprise, for she had been rehearsing what to say to start it all.

'You know Aunt Viola, Zoe?' he asked, his voice casual.

Zoe looked startled, her eyes going quickly round the group like those of a frightened animal. 'I ... I...'

'She doesn't know her,' her grandmother said. 'I saw to that.'

Zoe was biting her lip, still looking scared. Sheelagh decided this might be her chance.

'I expect she called for you at school, Zoe. It wasn't your fault.'

Turning quickly to Sheelagh, Zoe looked relieved. 'That's what she did. She waited outside the school gates and walked home most of the way with me.'

'Zoe love, why didn't you tell me?' Mrs Hamilton's voice was gentle.

'You'd have been cross, Gran. You always said I mustn't talk to strangers and though she said she was Aunty Viola, I didn't know her. And ... and she told me not to tell you 'cos if I did, you wouldn't let me go out to Daddy.'

'That's not true,' Mrs Hamilton began, but Tony gently lifted his hand.

'Did you like her, Zoe? Aunt Viola, I mean,' he asked.

Zoe shook her head violently. 'I hated her. She said Daddy was cruel.'

'That's a lie,' Sheelagh joined in angrily. 'She said that to me, too, but of course I didn't believe her.'

Zoe looked at her thoughtfully. 'Nor did I, but ... but then she said you killed Mummy, but then you said you were my age, so how could you?'

'Of course I couldn't. That just shows what lies she tells,' Sheelagh said.

Tony took a letter out of his pocket and opened it. 'This is what she wrote to me and the reason I'm here.' He looked at Luke, who was frowning. 'As Sheelagh may have told you, we grew up together and nearly married one another. Fortunately we didn't.' He smiled at Sheelagh. 'That's not meant as an insult, but we're both lucky enough to have found the right person. My wife and I were going over to England when this letter arrived.' He read the letter aloud in a silence that seemed to grow greater every moment:

'I am writing to you because I am so anxious about Sheelagh Tysack, who is now

Sheelagh Jessop. I know you two were very good friends, indeed nearly married, and there is no one else I can turn to for help. I know Sheelagh will never tell her parents about it in case it worries them, but she is in great trouble. The man she has married, Luke Jessop, has been married before. His wife died – it was all very hush-hush, but it was entirely due to his brutality and indifference. He also has a child whom he deserted and left to the grandparents to bring up. Sheelagh is living on a remote primitive island, with no friends. Her husband is a bully and I am afraid for her future. Please help her. I can think of no one else who could.'

'But it's not true!' Zoe cried out. 'Daddy didn't desert me.'

'Nor did he kill your mother,' Mrs Hamilton said angrily.

'It is all lies,' Luke agreed. He sounded weary, unusual for him Sheelagh thought worriedly, glancing across at him. 'She's just a perverted woman who can't help it. I appreciate your effort to come and rescue my wife.'

Tony grinned. 'I had a shock when I saw her at the airport. I've never seen her look so well or so happy. I must admit the letter worried me. It never struck me that it was a hoax.'

'What's a hoax?' Zoe asked. She jumped up and went to stand by her father, her face concerned. 'Don't worry, Daddy. We know it's not true, don't we?' She looked at Sheelagh and added: 'Sheelagh?'

Sheelagh felt a sudden unexpected feeling of joy. It was the first time Zoe had called her by name. Were they going to break down the barrier between them? She could be patient if she had some hope.

'Yes, Zoe, we know Daddy is a good kind man,' Sheelagh said quietly.

'A hoax,' Tony said, 'is not the right word in this case. A hoax is normally something done as a joke, but it can be dangerous. Like phoning a large hotel to say there's a bomb hidden in the cellar and having to hurry all the people out, often old, disabled folk, and then the phone goes again and someone laughs.'

Zoe nodded. 'I've read about that.'

'Actually this is worse, for this woman is deliberately trying to destroy your father's marriage,' Tony addressed himself to Zoe, speaking as to an adult. 'She's a jealous woman. You know what jealous is?'

'Yes. It's when you want someone belonging to someone else.'

How right she is, Sheelagh thought, her mouth curving into a little smile. If she had not been so convinced that Luke still belonged to Gina, everything would have been different.

'Well, it seems that Aunt Viola wanted to marry your daddy, but he married your mummy, so Aunt Viola hates him, and...'

'Wants to hurt him,' Zoe nodded again. She held out her hand to Tony. 'Can I see the letter?'

Tony gave it to her and she looked at it, then nodded again.

'Yes, it's her writing. The same as on Mummy's letters.'

'Mummy's letters?' Luke said quickly. 'Where did you find your mother's letters?' he asked, his voice stern.

Again Zoe had a frightened look as she stared round like a trapped animal.

'In my bottom drawer?' Sheelagh asked gently, and Zoe nodded.

'You had no right to read the letters...' Luke began, and turned to Sheelagh. 'I threw them away.'

'I rescued them,' Sheelagh said quietly. 'I had a feeling that one day we'd need them. I didn't read them, because they were not my mother's letters, but if Daddy died and I found letters of his or to him, I can't see why it would be wrong of me to read them. He's my father, just as … just as these letters were Zoe's mother's. They were from Aunty Viola, too, weren't they, Zoe?'

'The same writing. I'll get them. I've read them all,' Zoe added, looking at her father. 'They're terrible, but I don't believe them.'

She darted away and Luke looked at Sheelagh. 'Is this really necessary in front of Zoe?' he asked, his voice cold.

'I think it is, Luke. She's obsessed with the reason for her mother's death.'

Mrs Hamilton leant forward. 'But that's absurd! She knows her mother died of pneumonia.'

Zoe was back and put the small package on the round coffee table before Luke. 'Someone tore up Mummy's photo,' she said accusingly.

'It was an accident,' Sheelagh said quickly. 'I keep meaning to stick it together and have it framed.'

'Six letters?' Luke mused, frowning as he looked through them.

'They're all about the same thing, Daddy,' Zoe told him, leaning against his arm. 'She tells Mummy that she has a … a horrible disease that will kill her, but that you won't take her to a proper doctor, only to a ... a duck?' Zoe paused, her eyebrows lifting as she sought for the right word.

'Quack?' Tony suggested, and Zoe rewarded him with a smile.

'That's right. What's a quack?'

Luke was reading the letters quickly, passing each one on in turn to Sheelagh and Mrs Hamilton.

'A quack is what the doctors call a man who's not fully qualified,' Tony explained, and saw Zoe was still puzzled. 'He hasn't passed all his exams.'

'Am I a quack, then, because I don't pass my exams?' Zoe asked, her voice anxious.

Tony smiled. 'No – it only applies to doctors. So Aunt Viola said Daddy wouldn't take Mummy to a good doctor. Right?'

'That's right, and she keeps asking Mummy to go back to England before she dies so that they can save her life ... but she died, all the same.'

'Two years later, Zoe darling,' Mrs Hamilton said gently. 'She had no disease. She died of pneumonia. She was ill with it and as she was getting better, she was asked out to a dance. I begged her not to go, but she went and caught another cold. She was still weak from the first illness and that was why she died.'

'Because she went to a dance when she wasn't well?' Zoe looked puzzled.

'Pneumonia leaves you feeling very weak, Zoe,' Tony chimed in. 'In any case, if these lies of Aunt Viola had been true, your mother would have been in great pain and your granny would have known it.'

'But why did she write those letters to Mummy?' Zoe brushed back her fringe impatiently. 'If she was Mummy's best friend?'

'Because she wanted to break up your mother's marriage and make her hate and be afraid of your father,' Tony said. 'She was your mother's worst enemy, not her best friend.'

Mrs Hamilton looked very near tears. 'That explains so much,' she said slowly. 'I could never understand why Gina had become an absolute hypochondriac.' She turned to Zoe. 'That means someone who always thinks she is ill. We spent a fortune on doctors and specialists as she kept complaining and the X-rays and examinations could find nothing wrong, and then for a few weeks your mother would be as well as could be, really cheerful. Then she'd have another deep go of depression. I wonder if Viola went on writing to her in England.'

Luke had read the last letter as he passed it over. 'I don't know what to say – except perhaps poor Gina.'

'At least it wasn't your fault, Luke...' Sheelagh began, and Zoe chimed in.

'Nobody knowing you, Daddy, would believe that. Mummy must have had a funny mind. There are people like that, you know. Anyhow, I'm glad that's over.' She put her arms round Luke's neck and kissed him. 'I'll never believe nasty things of you, Daddy,' she promised, and looked across the room. 'Nor will Sheelagh, I know,' she added. 'I'm sleepy, so good night.'

Mrs Hamilton rose, too. 'I feel like bed. I am shocked, Luke, to think that any woman could behave like that Viola Whittaker. Something should be done about her. It may not be only you she's trying to hurt. Goodnight, everyone.' She paused by Sheelagh's chair, touched her hand and smiled. 'Bless you, my dear,' she said, her voice suddenly thickening as she left them.

'I don't see what we can do,' Luke sighed as he and Tony sat down again.

Tony nodded. 'I think I can help – not personally, but through a friend in London. We'll put the fear of being taken to court in her. I'm not sure what we could prove, but I think this type of woman would probably be scared stiff when faced with a solicitor's letter.'

'You think it might work?' Luke asked.

'We can have a try.' Tony stood up, yawning. 'Forgive me, it's been quite a day.' He smiled at them. 'Anyhow, anyone seeing you two together would know there's nothing wrong with your marriage. Did Sheelagh tell you we're expecting our first baby? I've brought my wife over to meet my parents, so I'll look in and see your folks, Sheelagh, and tell them how well and happy you are.'

'Thanks,' said Luke, standing up as well. 'I expect Sheelagh will be going herself soon. I'll give you a lift back.' He turned to the door and Sheelagh sat very still.

What had he meant? Was he going to send her back to her parents? Was their marriage completely wrecked? Suddenly she felt sick.

'Goodnight, Tony.'

'See you tomorrow before I go?' he asked, taking her hand in his.

'I expect so.'

'Of course,' Luke said. 'We'll drive you to the jetty and see you off. I'll be right back, Sheelagh,' he said, and the two men went off.

Slowly, Sheelagh went round, emptying ash trays, closing windows, tidying up, then she had a bath and got into bed. She tried not to look at her watch, but the hands moved round slowly as she waited and waited.

Was he going to spend tonight out as he had spent the night before? she wondered.

CHAPTER 11

Luke was not home by one o'clock and Sheelagh, sitting up in bed, pretending to read and trying not to watch the clock, was nearly mad with anxiety. She kept reminding herself of the thousands of reasons why Luke was not home. Mercury might have wanted to talk business – there might have been visitors there, too ... but surely, then, Luke would have phoned her? He could have had an accident, the cattle were apt to wander across the road and were difficult to see in the dark ... he might have had a puncture while driving fast and slid off the steep cliff-side road...

Suddenly she was sure of that. Luke was in trouble and needed her. She slid out of bed, pulling on a pair of yellow trews and a white shirt, hunting for the key of her little red car, and hurried outside. It was pitch dark, the moon having vanished behind some clouds, and the beam from her torch was not much help.

The night-watchman, a tall elderly man swinging a lantern in one hand and what looked like a heavy stick in the other came to her side.

'Madame is in trouble?' he asked in their strange French.

Wondering if she was making a great fuss about nothing, Sheelagh told him she was worried because her husband, the Monsieur, had not returned from Monsieur Mercury's house and that she was going to look for him. He nodded and guided her to where the car was parked, then stood back to watch her drive off.

There had been a lot more rain than she had realised, for when she had driven back that day from the jetty she had been too concerned with more important matters to have really noticed the weather, but now the clouds were threatening a storm and the distant rumbles of thunder and occasional forked slashes of lightning across the sky assured her the storm was on its way.

She drove slowly along. It was ten miles of mountainside as well as ocean-side, and she looked carefully in case Luke's car had skidded off the road. She felt wet with fear. Supposing he was hurt? Supposing that like poor Mrs Hamilton, she had lost her husband? Sheelagh shivered. No, she must be exaggerating. Luke was used to these roads, it was unlikely that he would have an accident ... he was a good driver and...

She caught her breath, for the long beam of the car's headlights had shown her a strange figure ahead. A tall man, splattered with mud, hopping along on one foot, pausing now as if for a rest...'

Speeding up the car, she hurried towards him, stopping alongside, almost falling out of the car in her eagerness, aware but uncaring that she was walking in deep mud.

'Luke darling, what's happened?' she exclaimed, going to his side. She had left the car door open to give her light, but it was hard to see his face.

'Nothing serious,' he told her, 'just that you've got the biggest idiot in the world for a husband.'

'I have!' She was so relieved that she wanted to cry. Now she held his arm tightly. 'Oh, Luke, I thought you were hurt!'

'So I am,' he said reprovingly. 'I think I've sprained my ankle. It's hurting like hell.'

'Come into the car and rest it. I'd better drive.' Sheelagh helped him hop round the car to the other door.

'I think so, too. I doubt if I could put this foot near the pedal.'

Sitting by his side, as she turned to look at him in the car's light, Sheelagh asked the questions that she was longing to ask, very aware that his arm was round her shoulders.

'What happened? I got so worried, and then I thought Mercury might be talking business and...'

'I'd have phoned you. No, simply as I said, you have the biggest idiot in the world for a husband. Pierre is a good chauffeur, but I ought to know by now, thoroughly unreliable. The other day we had a puncture and I told him to get the tyre mended. Tonight I was driving home when I nearly went into the ocean as the back wheel went. I got out.' He began to laugh, his arm round Sheelagh's shoulder tightened. 'Let this be a lesson, Sheelagh. I took off the wheel and went to get the spare tyre. It wasn't there!'

'Oh no...!'

'Oh yes. I was so mad, I stepped back without thinking and rolled down the side of the road, twisting my ankle badly. I lay there in the mud and swore at myself for not checking the car. Honestly, of all the idiots! Then I managed to climb up the bank and wondered what to do. I had the choice of sitting in the car until found – I was sure you'd be asleep – or hopping home. I didn't realise quite how exhausting hopping can be.'

'How could I sleep? I was worried about you.'

His hand squeezed her arm gently. 'Bless you, I should have known. Now as this is one hell of a road for turning round in the dark, I suggest we drive on to Mercury's and turn in the drive. Right?'

'As you say, monsieur,' Sheelagh joked. She was feeling so happy, for this was the Luke she had fallen in love with, this was the Luke she knew and loved.

She drove carefully through the mud until they came to Mercury's mansion, as she called it now, turning easily in the driveway, seeing a few lights were still on in the house.

Back along the road again she drove, and they talked a little.

'You think it's a good idea for Zoe to go to boarding school?' asked Luke.

Sheelagh nodded. 'I didn't at first. I wanted

her to live with us, but I think you're right and this is best for her.'

'We'll have her in the holidays,' Luke said. He turned to look at her. 'Sheelagh, I've so much to tell you. What say we park along here under the trees and have a talk? It's so much easier than at home.'

'Right. Tell me when.' Sheelagh tried to hide her delight. It was Luke who wanted to talk, this time. Maybe they would smooth out all their problems.

'Just along here ... stop...'

Sheelagh obeyed and the car slid off the road, luckily on to the smooth verge. 'Oh no!' Luke groaned. 'That makes two idiots in our family. I didn't mean you to stop *there*. I was going to say *stop by that great white stone.*'

'You said stop, and...' Sheelagh was battling with the car, but it had sunk deep in the mud, the wheels churning helplessly as she revved.

'It's hopeless,' Luke told her. 'We'll need a tractor to pull us out.'

'I'm sorry,' Sheelagh began, but Luke pulled her closer and kissed her.

'Don't be. I'm glad it isn't my arms that were hurt. I can hold you like this and tell you how much I love you.'

'Will you?' Sheelagh stroked his cheek. 'I

wish you'd tell me that every day.'

'Wouldn't you get bored?'

'Bored?' She began to laugh. 'You really are an idiot, Luke!'

'No regrets about Tony?' he asked. 'He seems a decent chap.'

'None at all, because I've got the nicest husband in the world.'

'And I have the nicest wife,' he said as he kissed her.

She knew he meant it. That no longer would she be jealous of Gina. Poor Gina who had let her life and marriage be destroyed by malicious Viola. Sheelagh shivered as she thought how nearly Viola had destroyed theirs.

'As soon as Mrs Hamilton and Zoe have gone back to England,' Luke said, 'we're going away.'

'Lovely. Where?'

'Rome, the Greek islands, maybe Austria … our honeymoon, love. Better late than never.'

'What fun, Luke! But I know now that wherever I go with you, it'll be a honeymoon.'

'I'll see to that,' he promised as he kissed her.

Suddenly she saw lights coming towards

them ... from in front and from behind.

'The watchman must have sent us help,' she said.

'Perhaps Mercury heard us turn and sent out to see,' Luke agreed. 'Oh, hell,' he sighed. 'Why won't people leave us alone?'

Sheelagh laughed. 'We've our life before us.'

'You're right,' he said. 'Together.'

'Together,' she repeated slowly. Surely, she thought, it was the most beautiful word in the world?

The publishers hope that this book has given you enjoyable reading. Large Print Books are especially designed to be as easy to see and hold as possible. If you wish a complete list of our books please ask at your local library or write directly to:

Dales Large Print Books
Magna House, Long Preston,
Skipton, North Yorkshire.
BD23 4ND

This Large Print Book, for people
who cannot read normal print,
is published under the auspices of

THE ULVERSCROFT FOUNDATION

... we hope you have enjoyed this book.
Please think for a moment about those
who have worse eyesight than you ...
and are unable to even read or enjoy
Large Print without great difficulty.

You can help them by sending a
donation, large or small, to:

**The Ulverscroft Foundation,
1, The Green, Bradgate Road,
Anstey, Leicestershire, LE7 7FU,
England.**
or request a copy of our brochure for
more details.

The Foundation will use all donations
to assist those people who are visually
impaired and need special attention
with medical research, diagnosis
and treatment.

Thank you very much for your help.